KT-450-493
Bristol Libraries
1806256851

Books by Candy Guard

Turning to Jelly

Jelly Has a Wobble

Jelly Breaks the Mould

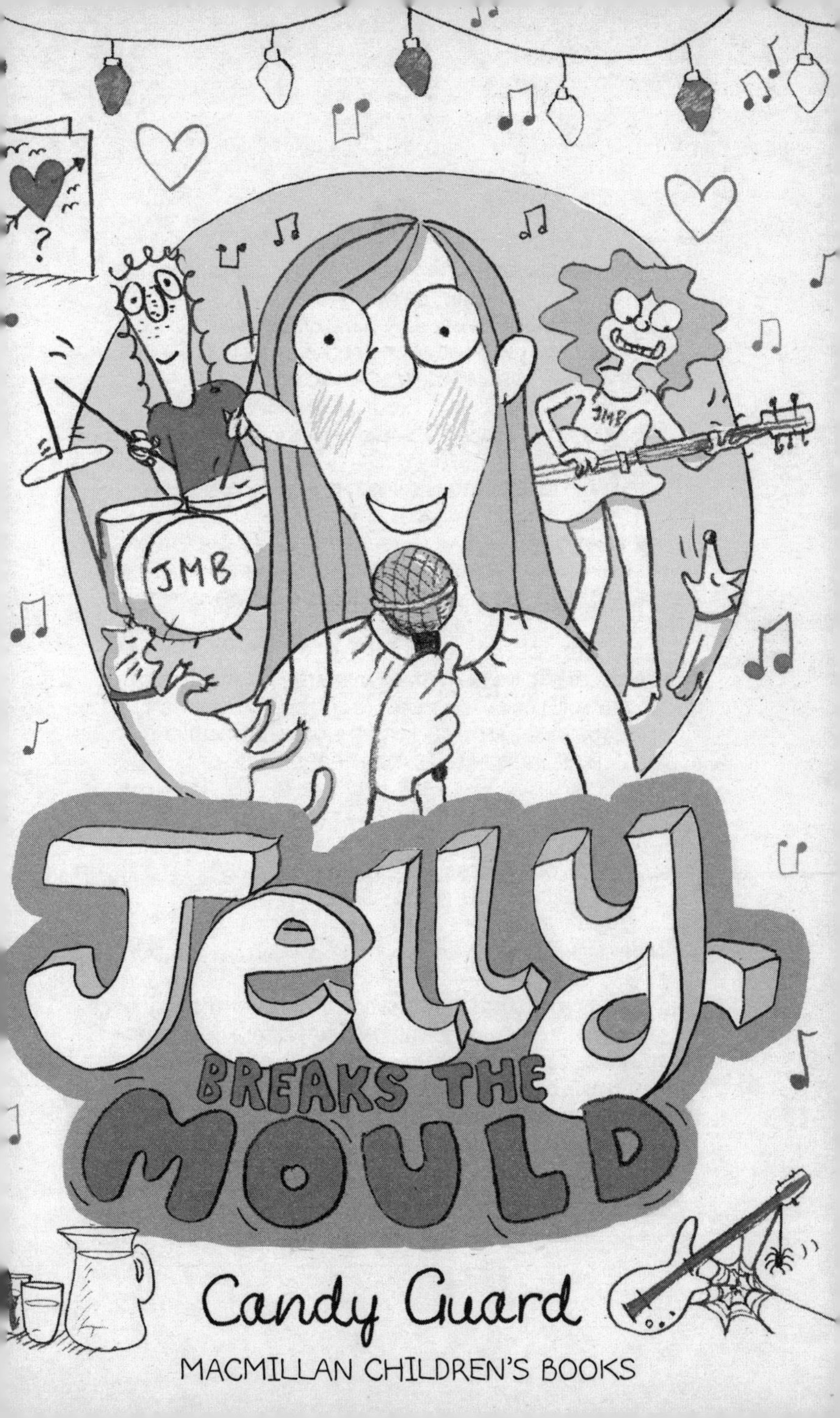
JMB
JMB
JMB
Jelly
BREAKS THE
MOULD
Candy Guard
MACMILLAN CHILDREN'S BOOKS

FIRST PUBLISHED 2016 BY MACMILLAN CHILDREN'S BOOKS
AN IMPRINT OF PAN MACMILLAN
20 NEW WHARF ROAD, LONDON N1 9RR
ASSOCIATED COMPANIES THROUGHOUT THE WORLD
WWW.PANMACMILLAN.COM

ISBN 978-1-4472-5616-8

TEXT AND ILLUSTRATIONS COPYRIGHT © CANDY GUARD 2016

THE RIGHT OF CANDY GUARD TO BE IDENTIFIED AS THE AUTHOR AND ILLUSTRATOR OF THIS WORK HAS BEEN ASSERTED BY HER IN ACCORDANCE WITH THE COPYRIGHT, DESIGNS AND PATENTS ACT 1988.

ALL RIGHTS RESERVED. NO PART OF THIS PUBLICATION MAY BE REPRODUCED, STORED IN A RETRIEVAL SYSTEM, OR TRANSMITTED, IN ANY FORM OR BY ANY MEANS (ELECTRONIC, MECHANICAL, PHOTOCOPYING, RECORDING OR OTHERWISE), WITHOUT THE PRIOR WRITTEN PERMISSION OF THE PUBLISHER.

1 3 5 7 9 8 6 4 2

A CIP CATALOGUE RECORD FOR THIS BOOK IS AVAILABLE FROM THE BRITISH LIBRARY.

PRINTED AND BOUND BY CPI GROUP (UK) LTD, CROYDON CR0 4YY

THIS BOOK IS SOLD SUBJECT TO THE CONDITION THAT IT SHALL NOT, BY WAY OF TRADE OR OTHERWISE, BE LENT, RESOLD, HIRED OUT, OR OTHERWISE CIRCULATED WITHOUT THE PUBLISHER'S PRIOR CONSENT IN ANY FORM OF BINDING OR COVER OTHER THAN THAT IN WHICH IT IS PUBLISHED AND WITHOUT A SIMILAR CONDITION INCLUDING THIS CONDITION BEING IMPOSED ON THE SUBSEQUENT PURCHASER.

For my amazing stepdaughters,
Rosie, Heather and Robin,
who actually **are** musical

–1–

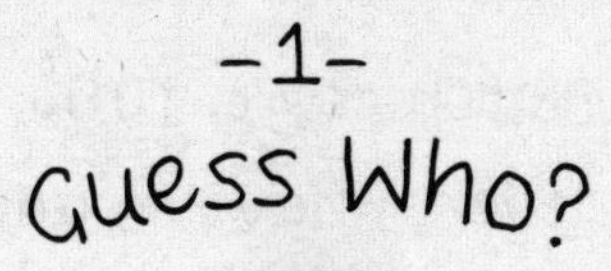

Today is Valentine's Day and I have a card! It was on my bed when I got back from school. It said 'Jelly' on the front of the envelope in my mum's handwriting . . .

It wasn't very romantic . . .

Inside it said . . .

But Sandy Blatch can't *fool* me!! He has been very clever, I have to admit.

He has copied my mum's handwriting perfectly, and pretending it was from our dog, Fatty, was genius (Mum always does me a card from Fatty). I'm not sure how Sandy got into our house to leave it on the bed but I know he is very good with a l o n g ladder and an open window from the time he rescued Mum from the Room of Doom when she got locked in there during my party.

Mum **winked** at me when I went downstairs.

Aren't you going to give your true love your answer?

Very good, Mum.

THEN I called a Faithful Club meeting at our headquarters (the shed in my garden) so I could show off about my card. The Faithful Club has been going since junior school but as it is a bit **embarrassing** to still have a club at Big School it is now a *secret club*. The members are me, my best friends Myf and Roobs and my neighbour Ricky Chin (occasional boy member – he only comes when there are biscuits).

Myf and Roobs were *extremely* jealous of my card because neither of them had got one . . . EVER.

Isn't that your mum's writing, Jelly?
That's definitely Fatty's paw print.
Shuddup, jealous.

How could Sandy leave it on your bed? He was at school all day.
It's not very romantic – luv 'n' liks?
Why can't you just accept it's from Sandy?

-2-

Gooseberry Fools

The next day at school I was wandering along the corridor with Myf and Roobs feeling NERVOUS and excited that I might see Sandy.

'Look, Jelly,' Myf shouted, pointing at a poster. 'Sandy's band's playing!'

Myf is fairly untalented at most things but she is VERY good at shouting.

sO.M.G.!
LIVE GIG!
IN FRONT
OF OUR
HOME CROWD
FRIDAY 6 P.M.

Sandy Blatch sings and plays keyboards in **sO.M.G.!** (an **O.M.G.!** tribute band). **O.M.G.!** had been our **FAVOURITE** band (along with six million other *silly* girls) – but since Buster Bauble (the lead singer and Sandy look-a-like) had left to go solo **O.M.G.!** had got a bit rubbish and we went off them a bit. Buster Bauble's solo career hadn't worked out and he'd gone a bit *wild* then sunk into obscurity. And then **O.M.G.!** had split up.

We were standing staring at the poster when Sandy suddenly appeared beside us.

Oh, hi, Sandy! Jelly's really pleased with her Valentine's Day card.

Is she? Who does she think it's from?

You of course! Durr brain.

Well, I – err . . . ooh . . . I didn't realise it was Valentine's Day till I got this.

I was hoping it was from you, Jelly.

NO! That's Cicily Fanshaw's writing! I know because I copy her in Geography . . .

That was annoying – Cicily Fanshaw is the most competitive girl in the school.

Even though she was small she always won everything by sheer determination – running races, the shot-put, the high jump, the triple jump – and now she was interested in boys she was probably going to apply the same willpower to that.

I felt a little anxious. She would probably try to steal Sandy away from me. (Not that he was really mine to begin with.)

After Sandy's band did the music at my mum's wedding at the end of the summer and Sandy had admired my ears and pretty much said he liked me, I'd gone very **embarrassed** and made a muck-up of everything. The first week back at school for the autumn term I kept surreptitiously **looking** around for him . . .

. . . and whenever I saw his scarf out of the corner of my eye (it was very bright and stripy) I would studiously look at ANYTHING rather than HIM.

And if I saw his scarf coming my way I would turn on my heels and hurry off . . .

Then one day Sandy's best friend and guitarist in sO.M.G.!, Benji Butler, caught me coming out of the girls' toilets and presented me with THE SCARF!

I went extremely **red** but took the scarf and gave him mine (slightly wishing I hadn't wiped poached egg off my chin with it earlier at breakfast).

I hurried off to a dark corner of the corridor and sniffed it – it smelt of Sandy.

At our school, wearing each other's scarves means you are 'going out' with each other, which very rarely means going out anywhere, or staying in anywhere, or in fact even speaking to each other. But Sandy had other ideas – he actually did seem to want to go out with me. Every few weeks he would have another bash, but I always made an excuse and said no.

UNSURPRISINGLY, after a few months he slightly gave up and cooled off, though we were still wearing each other's scarves. And then of course I DEEPLY regretted being so shy and wished I'd said yes at least once.

But now Sandy said,

Anyway, I'm glad I ran into you, Jelly. I was wondering if you'd like to come to our gig on Friday?

A date! He was asking me on another date!

So this time instead of saying 'No', out of embarrassment, like I normally would, I said 'Yes' in an **embarrassed** way.

Roobs said, 'I suppose no one's interested in an O.M.G.! tribute band now the real O.M.G.! have split up?'

‘Well . . .’ Sandy smiled. ‘We’ve got a small local following of ex-O.M.G.! fans who come along to our gigs.’

And why don’t you two come as well?
No, they don’t want to come!

Yes we do!

Great!

he said, and walked off whistling.

See you at the gig, Sandy!

I pretended to be annoyed that Myf and Roobs had invited themselves on *my* date, but really I was relieved.

What if Sandy took me somewhere afterwards? Or walked me home? He might **kiss** me. I went **red** just thinking about it.

-3-
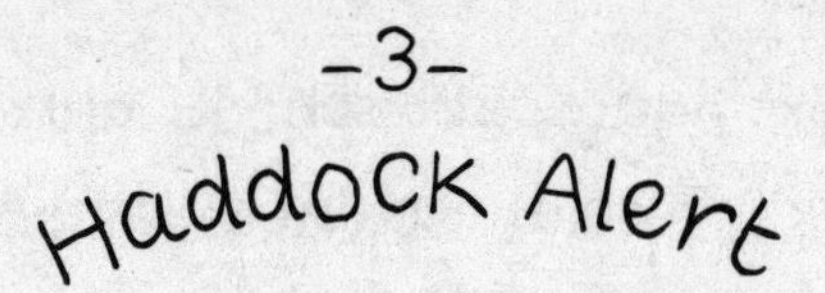

I had trouble sleeping that night and started feeling less confident about my Valentine's Day card. I decided there was a very teeny SLIGHT chance that it WAS from my mum via the dog.

The next day at school during Miss Haddock's Social Science lesson I also started feeling unsure about my 'date' . . .

Did Sandy just want a rent-a-crowd? No, don't be silly! He was just being polite to Myf and Roobs – he and I will meet afterwards and hang out. It's going to be great! (As long as he doesn't try to kiss me.)

Don't write on the desk, Jellifer!!!!

I started with a jolt and looked up. Miss

Haddock was standing over me. I'd been so lost in thought I'd been doodling on the desk without realising. She always calls me Jellifer because of a misunderstanding on the first day of secondary school . . .

Name?

Jelly Rowntree.

Jenny?

No, **Jelly**.

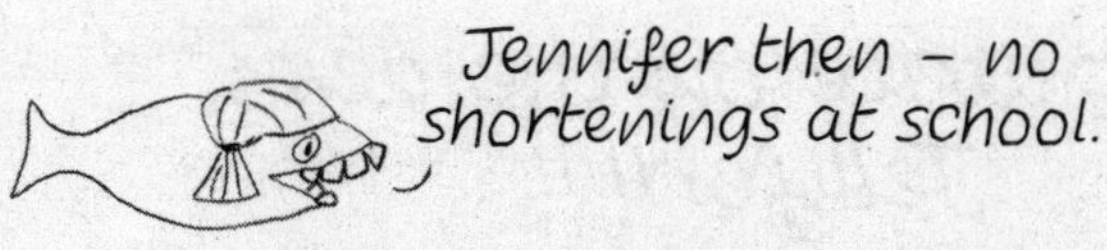

Jennifer then – no shortenings at school.

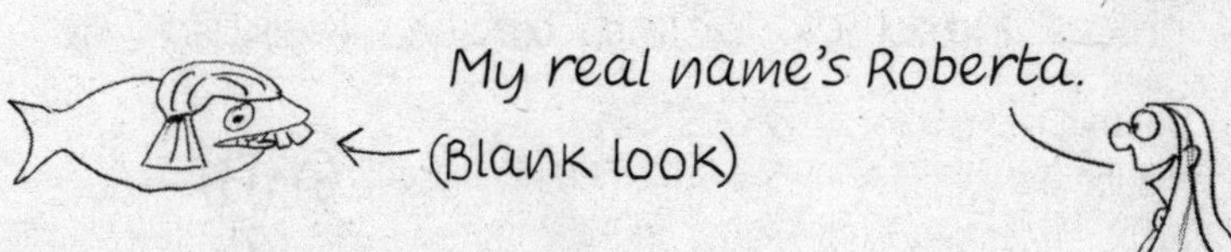

My real name's Roberta.
(Blank look)

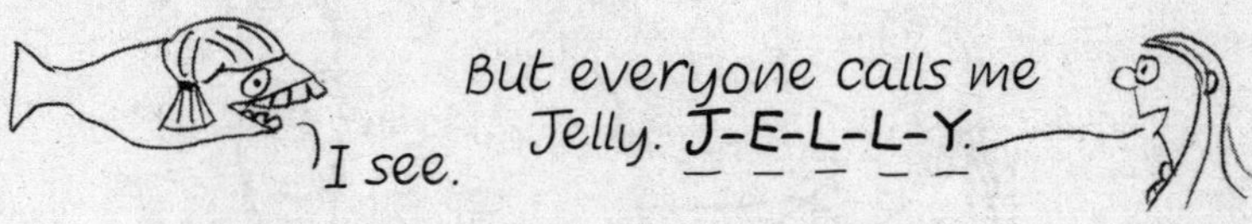

But everyone calls me Jelly. J-E-L-L-Y.
I see.

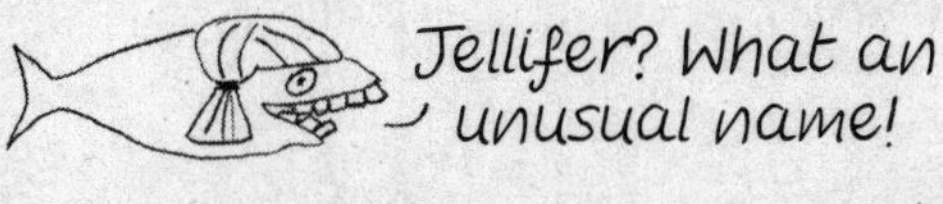

Jellifer? What an unusual name!

But . . .

One more peep out of you and it's twice round the playing field!

'Hmph,' she grunted now and continued droning. 'So if the law states that you must pay certain taxes . . .'

I mean . . . maybe I should go to the gig on my own? Myf and Roobs will just cramp my style. I'll tell them . . .

Don't write on the desk, Jellifer!!!!!

Miss Haddock yelled again, making me jump out of my skin.

Sorry, Miss!

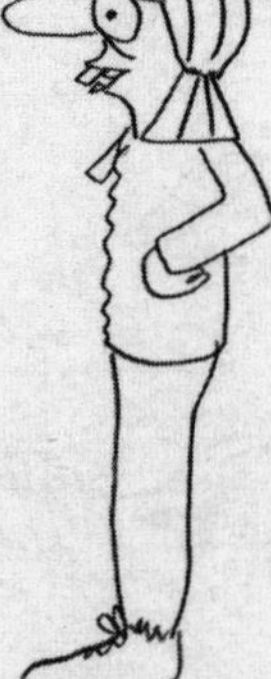

I sat up and tried to look alert.

But the next thing I knew, I was absorbed in my own thoughts and doodling on the desk again . . .

I wonder if that card was from Cicily Fanshaw? I . . .

DON'T WRITE ON THE DESK, JELLIFER!!!!

You don't write on the furniture at home, do you, Jellifer? That's a double detention for you.

I already had a detention for being loud earlier in my favourite lesson, BIOLOGY, with my FAVOURITE teacher, Miss Jasmine. Unfortunately, I'm NOT her favourite pupil.

I've sat on the sheep's backbone!
I've sat on the sheep's backbone!

Jelly! Why is it always your voice I can hear above everyone else's?
OUT!

But, Miss, I was just being enthusiastic.

-4-
Sin Bin

We had to do detentions in a room everyone called the Sin Bin. Today it was just me and Sonja Perkins, the most frightening girl in the school – rap fan, arm-wrestling champion and general SCARY person.

On duty in the Sin Bin today was the Nicest Teacher in the Whole School: Mrs Lilac. Mrs Lilac was *always* nice and NEVER lost her temper, was *never* sarcastic OR irritable.

Even the average very, very, VERY nice person is a bit not very nice *sometimes.* They might release a small tut or wrinkle their brow into a minuscule frown or eject an almost silent sigh – or *something.*

But Mrs Lilac **NEVER** tutted or sighed or frowned. She was always, always, ALWAYS nice – and everyone was nice back.

It would be **embarrassing** not to be.

The thought of Mrs Lilac's hurt face looking back at you if you were anything but NICE was enough to put even the meanest person off being mean. Or the thought of her not REALISING you weren't being nice and being SUPER NICE back, beaming her big **innocent** smile at you, would make you shrivel with shame.

Mrs Lilac was the Drama teacher and when she walked in it was impossible for Sonja and I to keep up our sulky posturing.

Hello, Jelly darling!
Hello, Sonja dear!
How LOVELY to see you both! Why on earth are you two angels in this dreadful place??
Loud and writing on desk, Mrs Lilac.
Loud and using phone, Mrs Lilac.
Ah, well they don't sound like such terrible things! Just natural high spirits in lovely young girls!
Yes, Mrs Lilac.

After about ten minutes of Mrs Lilac smiling indulgently at us and us staring back with fixed grins, Mrs Lilac cleared her throat.

'Loudness, liveliness, high spirits – we should be harnessing all that wonderful energy – have either of you thought of going on the stage?'

Neither of us responded, but just carried on grinning.

'I wonder if you – both of you – would consider auditioning for the school play? I think you both have raw talent, stage presence, an unassuming natural beauty and an emotional depth to your voices.'

We were both STUNNED. Neither of us had EVER had so many compliments in a short space of time – in fact I'd only ever had seven and Sonja had only ever had three.........

The First Compliment I Can Remember:

Age: 3½

Hasn't Roberta got lovely blue eyes!
(Hilda, our old babysitter)

Amount Of Time I Thrived On Compliment:

Nine Years

Age: 3½ → Age: 12½

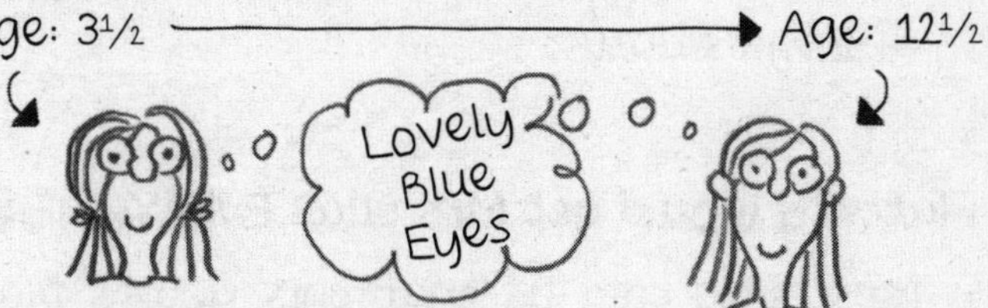

My Other Compliments:

2) 'You have excellent eye/hand co-ordination.' (Unknown ping-pong player on holiday)
3) 'Jelly's very dextrous.' (Julian)
4) 'You have fine hair but there's a lot of it.' (Sharon – hairdresser)
5) 'Hair like flowing silk.' (Sandy Blatch)
6) 'Cute ears.' (Sandy Blatch)

7) 'You really know how to throw a stylish outfit together, Jelly!' (Julian)

Sonja's compliments:

1) 'Wonderful colouring.' (Auntie Wanda)
2) 'Your bread rolls are the best in the class, Sonja.' (Mrs Cripps, cookery teacher)
3) 'She's as strong as an ox, my Sonja.' (Sonja's dad)

Flattery would get Mrs Lilac EVERYWHERE.

Mrs Lilac told us that this year's play was *Romeo and Juliet* by William Shakespeare and that the auditions were in two days' time. Sonja and I smiled at each other and said we would both be there.

Me and Sonja Perkins!! Bonding!! She was a very COOL person to have as a friend.

Mrs Lilac said we could leave our

detention early as we had been such lovely girls. We said our goodbyes and as we left the classroom I said to Sonja, 'I don't know *Romeo and Juliet* at all, do you?' and she said, 'Shuddup, Jelly, else I'll whack you one.'

'OK, bye!' I said back, smiling, and we both waved to Mrs Lilac who was waving to us through the window, and went our separate ways, Sonja throwing a rubber at me – quite **hard** – once we were out of Mrs Lilac's sight.

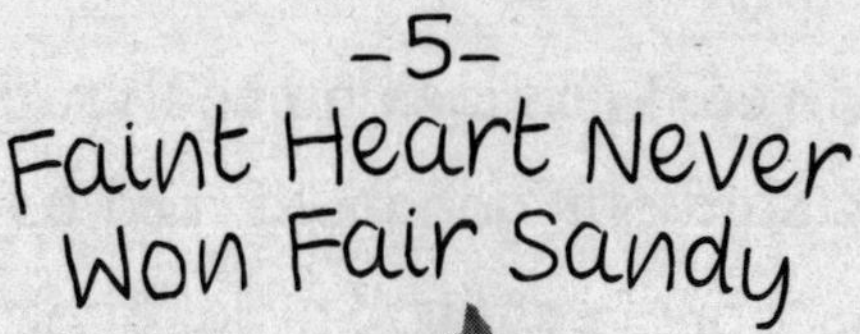

-5- Faint Heart Never Won Fair Sandy

Although I knew it was a date and Sandy had only invited Myf and Roobs to be polite, and even though they were being completely immature and pretending to be French on the bus . . .

I let them come to the gig to support Sandy and his band as obviously hardly anyone would be there oooooooo

However, when we got to Boxford Town Hall, it was heaving with screaming girls.

sO.M.G.! hadn't built up a small following of ex-O.M.G.! fans – they'd built up a MASSIVE following of ex-O.M.G.! fans. It seemed Sandy Blatch's squeaky clean image was helping them with the disappointment of the real Buster Bauble's grubby downfall. Sandy reminded them of the old Buster. They had all adapted their O.M.G.! T-shirts by adding an S at the beginning and turning them into sO.M.G.! T-shirts.

As I was more or less Sandy's girlfriend, I didn't need to *rush* towards the stage when they came on. I just stood at the back, casually sipping my Coke and flaunting Sandy's stripy scarf. Myf and Roobs (being silly, immature and boyfriend-less) joined in with all the other BaubleBelles (now BlatchBabes) singing along and screaming.

Sandy spotted me and was definitely singing the more romantic numbers whilst staring at me.

Then I heard one girl say to another, 'He's singing to me!'

'No,' another retorted, 'he was singing to ME!'

'Anyway,' another one chipped in, 'he was looking right into MY eyes when he sang "A Heart Like Yours".'

'Rubbish!' another one piped up. 'He was looking at ME when he sang "Short Girl"!'

They were all so DELUDED!

'No, girls, it's ME he's looking at – Sandy's always had a soft spot for me!'

But sadly that wasn't ME shouting – I was too busy choking on the straw in my glass of Coke. It was Cicily Fanshaw, wearing a brightly coloured stripy scarf very much like the one Sandy had given me . . . I looked down at myself . . . It WAS my scarf! She had managed to slip it off my shoulders!

Faint heart never won fair maiden, Jelly.
What?

As Elizabeth the First said to Sir Francis Drake –

Who?

Or, as we say in Latin, Fortes fortuna adjuvat.

It means 'fortune favours the bold', Thicky.

I –

Basically, Jelly, if you really want something, you have to go for it! See ya!

After **S.O.M.G.!**'s last number I went backstage to find Sandy – but there was a HUGE crowd and he was right in the middle of it. I waved and he smiled and waved back.

Then I noticed a crowd of girls around me all waving too and I heard one girl say to another, 'He just waved at me!'

'No!' another one cried. 'He waved at me!'

'No! You lot are so deluded – Sandy more or less invited me on a date to this gig and he was waving at *me*!'

But again, unfortunately, that wasn't ME shouting – but Cicily! All Sandy had done was tell her where to buy the tickets and *she* had deluded herself into thinking it was a date!!!!

'Out the way, losers!' she yelled, and started pushing her way through the throng of girls.

Just as I was considering shoving through the crowd to speak to Sandy before Cicily got there – or, even better, cheating (like I'd done when I beat her in the CROSS COUNTRY! by going through the woods) and going round the outside of the throng and pushing in behind him, Myf and Roobs said they were fed up with waiting to speak to the boys.

'They've got all these groupies – we might as well go!' Myf shouted.

'Hang on . . .' I began. But then I saw Sandy was having yet *another* selfie taken with yet *another* groupie, and there were at least **fifty** girls still crowded round him. I tried to get his attention by waving, but the current groupie taking a selfie with Sandy was CICILY FANSHAW. As Sandy smiled sweetly into the camera, Cicily turned and poked her tongue out at me.

I suddenly had a very faint heart and felt I would NEVER **WIN** fair Sandy.

At the bus stop, Myf said,

I think WE should start a band! We can enter the Boxford's Got Talent contest! Then we might get loads of groupies too.

Boys don't be groupies, though, do they?

Of course they do!

They will when they see our band, anyway!

What about when they hear us?

I pointed out.

Having loads of groupies is quite dangerous.

I mean, you saw what it was like in there, there could easily be a stampede and you'd only have to lose your footing and fall over and you'd be trampled to death!

Myf and I left a respectful

p a u s e

for all those people crushed to death in Roobs's imagination before continuing, 'We could be a glam rock girl band!'

'Or an R'n'B soul band?!' I added, forgetting about our lack of musical ability.

'Or an indie girl guitar band!' Roobs cried, forgetting about all the flattened people.

'I think we should be a punk band,' Myf said firmly.

'No,' Roobs said.

We were already having "musical" differences, which meant we were a proper band. We were SO EXCITED we decided to have a Faithful Club meeting first thing in the morning.

-6- All About the Bass

Roobs had her clipboard out.

Right, what shall we call ourselves?
Er . . .
Um . . .
The Curtains?
The Clipboards?
The Fatties?
The Floor?

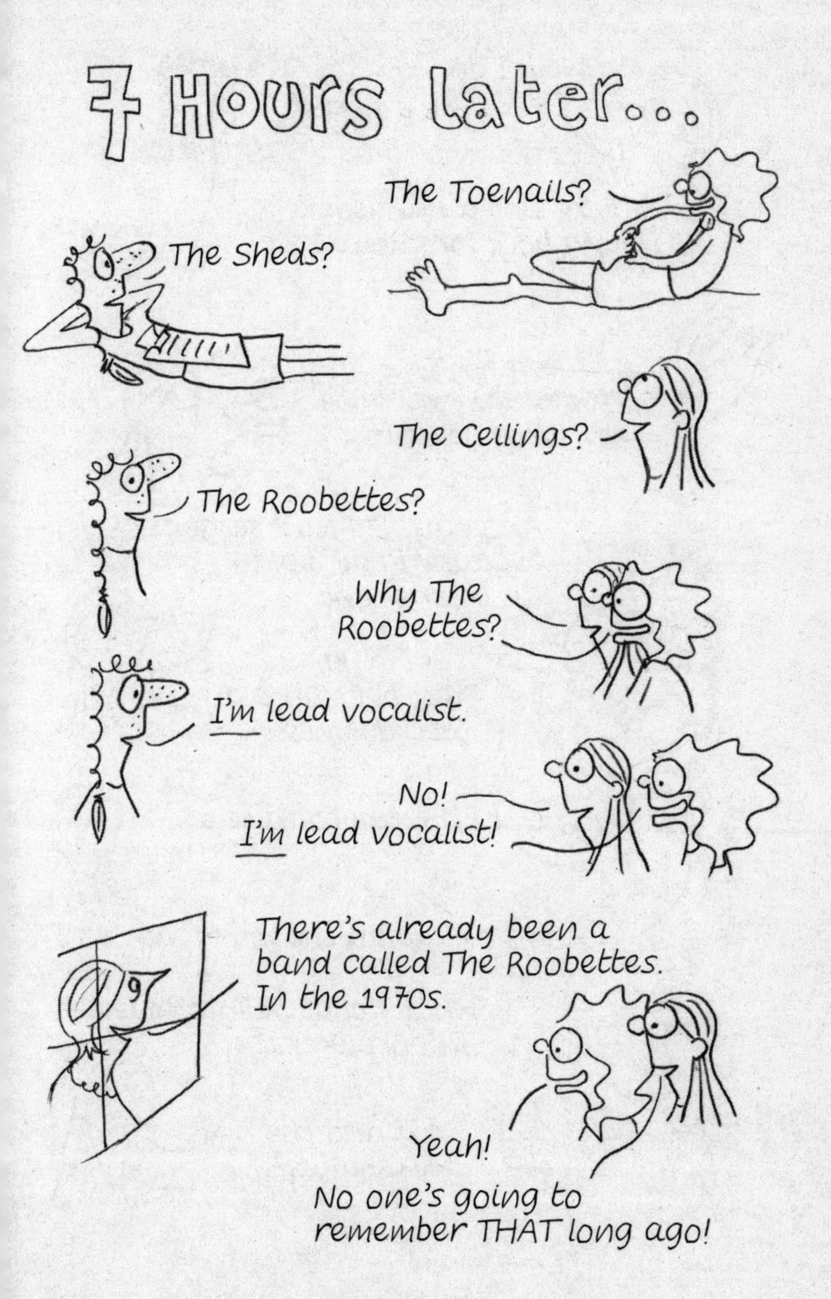
7 Hours later...
The Toenails?
The Sheds?
The Ceilings?
The Roobettes?
Why The Roobettes?
I'm lead vocalist.
No! I'm lead vocalist!
There's already been a band called The Roobettes. In the 1970s.
Yeah!
No one's going to remember THAT long ago!

Well, I do.

You're not a handsome young boy, Mrs Rowntree.

Too right.

Trying to be offended about not being a handsome young boy.

Anyway, I'M lead singer because I can't play an instrument . . .

. . . or sing.

Yes, but YOU play instruments.

Only the tambourine . . .

And I only play the maracas . . .

What about Jelly and the Jail Breakers?

Mmm.

Myf and the Milkshakes?

I know! Jelly and the Mould Breakers!!!!
Myf and the Mould Breakers!
What's Myf got to do with mould?
MYF AND THE MOULD BREAKERS!!!!!!
No. Jelly and the Mould Breakers – else you're not having any crisps.
Myf and the Crisps? Come on – that's good!

Mrs Lilac's comments about my resonant voice, stage presence and natural beauty had gone to my head.

I don't know what Myf's excuse was.

We hadn't got any instruments yet so we improvised with biscuit tins, a tennis racquet and a hair brush. We sounded pretty good, considering, and we started feeling quite confident. After five minutes we were exhausted, though, so we decided to start designing our costumes. We got my mum's sewing box out – which had a pile of sewing from the last decade all wrapped up in a huge knot of different-coloured cotton threads – none of which seemed to lead to anything.

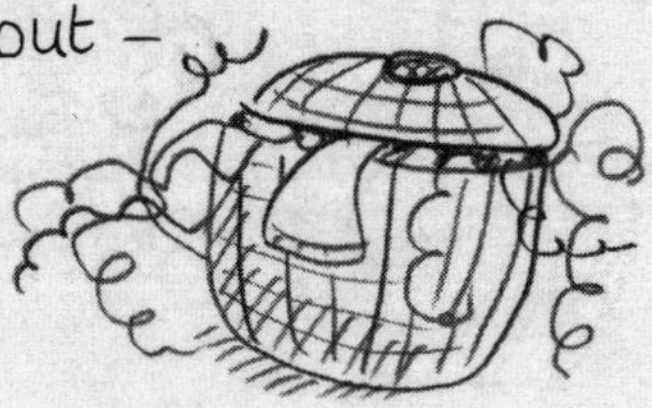

Mum had said,

I must do that sewing!

once a month since I can remember. At the bottom of the sewing basket was:

a pair of age five denim shorts of mine waiting for a new zip

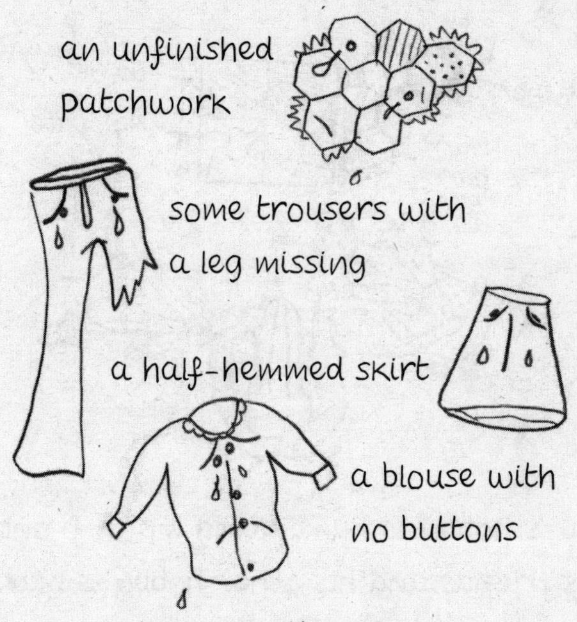

and many other heartbroken
and abandoned items of clothing.

We decided to use our Barbie dolls as models and use the material to design miniature outfits that might work for our band . . . but then we heard some 'sniggering' coming from the garden. It was my older brother, Jay, accompanied by his very handsome but dim friend Roger Lovely, my ex-crush.

Jay's hobby is humiliating me in front of his friends and his other hobby is making up *Stupid* songs about me.

It doesn't help that Myf and Roobs go very silly and giggly whenever Jay appears, which only encourages him.

Hee, hee! Hello, Jay.
We're starting a band!
What a stupid idea.
We're NOT starting a band.
Stop showing off in front of Roger, Jelly.
I'm NOT.

Well, I think it's a brilliant idea – there aren't enough girl bands.

It was MY idea, Roger.
I'm lead vocalist . . . but we haven't got any instruments yet.

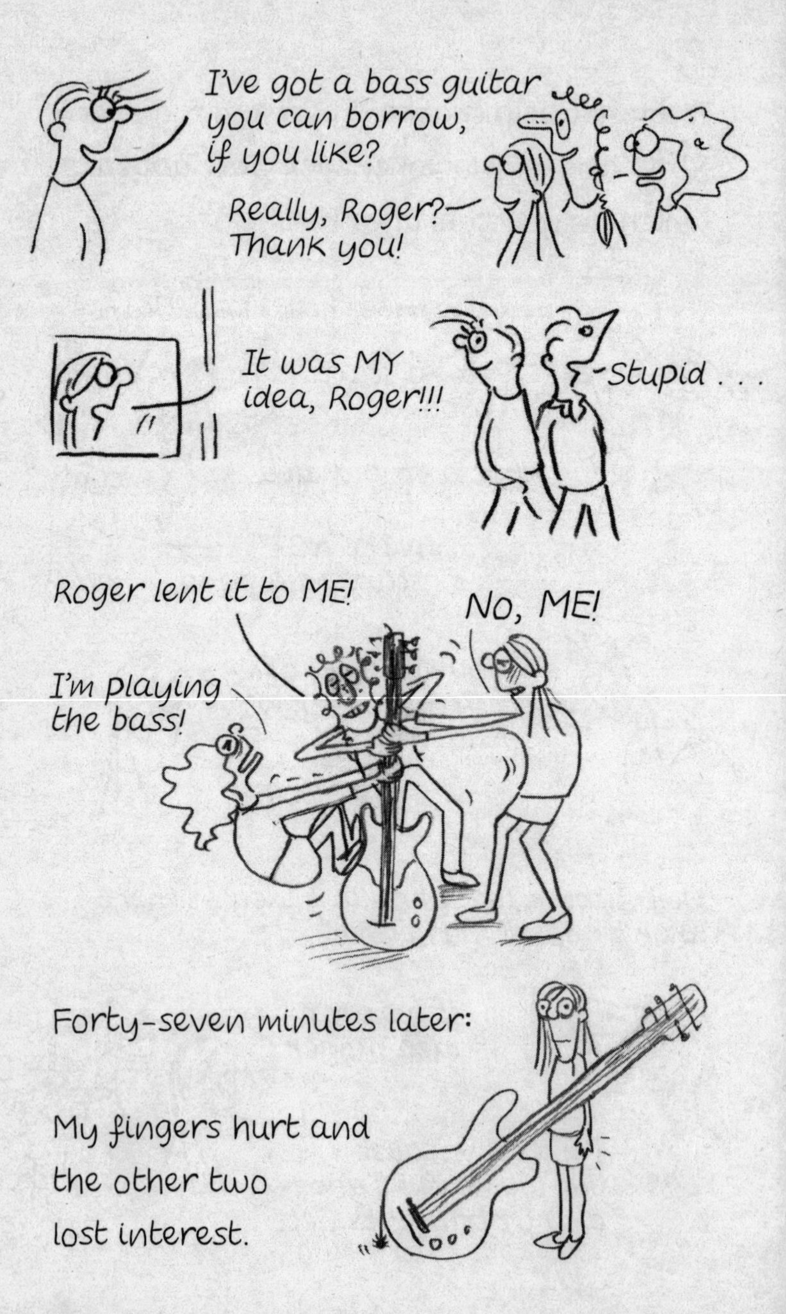
I've got a bass guitar you can borrow, if you like?
Really, Roger? Thank you!
It was MY idea, Roger!!!
Stupid . . .
Roger lent it to ME!
No, ME!
I'm playing the bass!
Forty-seven minutes later:
My fingers hurt and
the other two
lost interest.

Anyway, we had badges to make, costumes to design and posters to print.

Then my phone pinged. It was Sandy.

SANDY
Why didn't you turn up on Friday?
X X X

He **obviously** hadn't even noticed whether I was there! Let alone stared at me whilst singing the love songs!

'THE PIG!' I said to Myf and Roobs. 'We WERE just a rent-a-crowd.'

'That's a bit unfair to Sandy – they didn't really need a rent-a-crowd, did they?' Roobs said kindly. 'They already had a big crowd.'

'Hmph,' I replied, working out several replies to his text but then deciding to be an ICE queen and not answer at all. I decided that I liked Roger Lovely again and that I now had a crush on *him*.

-7-
Scarf Wars

At school on Monday I was putting our names down for Boxford's Got Talent (which wasn't for two months – plenty of time for us to learn instruments!) when Myf pointed to the poster about the auditions for *Romeo and Juliet*.

Come on, let's audition! They always have a brilliant party after the school play!

I think I'll audition for the part of the Nurse – there's only one other person auditioning.

Yeah, and its Sonja Perkins!

So? I'm not scared of Sonja Perkins!

Then **Roger Lovely** came along,

'Hi, Jells, how're you getting on with the bass?'

'Er, fine,' I said, going **scarlet** as usual.

'She hasn't even picked it up, Rog.'

'Yes, I have! Shuddup, Myf!'

Then, just as I was about to shuffle away, Mrs Lilac came floating along. 'Jelly daaarling! Hello, Roger luuurve! Myfanwy! How lovely to see you!'

Oh! I have just had a vision! You, Roger, could be my Romeo! Oh, definitely! You have the gentle nature, the youthful good looks, the strength of character. Oh, please audition! And, Jelly – my Juliet! That stage presence, wonderful diction, delicate features, rosy cheeks . . .

You are the perfect couple!!

She turned to Myf . . .

And Myfanwy, the charming, lovable, witty Myf – my Nurse! Diminutive in stature but strong and wilful in nature – you have the maturity to take the role, my darling.

with laughter.

'So, Roger,' Mrs Lilac said. 'Do you think you would like to play Romeo in *Romeo and Juliet*?'

Roger looked a bit confused.

'I don't understand, Mrs Lilac,' he said.

Did I mention that Roger had been kept back two years at school for being ~~handsome~~ THICK? Even Myf was more proficient in the brain department.

'It's a PLAY,' Myf explained to Roger as though Roger was a very small child, 'and Mrs Lilac wants you to play a PART in it.'

'OK!' he said, and wrote his name down.

He went off humming and I noticed he had written his name under Juliet so I went to cross it out and move it. It was then that I saw that Sandy had put his name down for Romeo . . .

And that Cicily Fanshaw had put her name down for Juliet! I felt my blood boiling and immediately wrote my name down as well. Cicily wasn't going to steal Sandy off me that easily! (Not that I cared.)

ROMEO
SANDY BLATCH
ROGER LOVELY
JULIET
CICILY FANSHAW
JESSICA WAINRIGHT
CARA SMITH
~~ROGER LOVELY~~
JELLY ROWNTREE
NURSE
SONJA PERKINS
(IF ANYONE ELSE AUDITIONS I'LL WHACK THEM)
MYFANWY HUGHES

'Look, Jelly, it's Sandy!' Myf shouted.

I immediately felt NERVOUS because I hadn't seen Sandy since the gig and I hadn't answered his text and I was worried he would mention our date or non-date or whatever it was and I was in a very going-red sort of mood.

'Hi, Jelly,' Sandy said, all *innocent* like he hadn't done anything wrong. 'Mrs Lilac's persuaded me to audition for Romeo even though I haven't got time now we've got so many gigs – but you know what she's like . . .'

'Hmm,' I murmured grumpily.

'Why didn't you come to see the band the other night?' he asked.

I noticed that he was still wearing my scarf and that he was looking at my neck where his scarf used to be and I went bright **red**.

Jelly said you just wanted a rent-a-crowd and that you were a pig.

Sandy looked a bit hurt.

'Shuddup, Myf!' I told her.

'So you just left?' he said. 'Without saying hello?'

'Well there were all these groupies; I couldn't get near you,' I said, noting that he was still wearing my scarf, but slightly tucked in his jacket.

'We want loads of groupies, don't we, Jelly?!' Myf yelled. 'That's why we're starting a band so we can get loads and LOADS of boyfriends!'

'I . . .' Sandy began.

Then suddenly Cicily materialised beside Sandy – wearing his scarf! – and started dragging him off.

Come on, Sandy, why don't we go and rehearse for the audition together!
I was just going to ask Jelly something . . . JELLY!

I was so **red** and flustered I just walked away.

I heard Sandy saying to Cicily, 'Where did you get that scarf?' and Cicily answering, 'Oh, Jelly threw it on the floor at your gig so I picked it up.'

'It's mine,' Sandy told her.

'Oh is it?! Here, you can wear mine if you like – it's Fanshaw tartan . . . no, not on top of that old rag, throw that away – it looks like it's got old egg on it . . .'

I glanced back to see that though Sandy was allowing Cicily to put her scarf round his neck, he was clutching my one firmly to his chest. He shot me a

confused look and I turned away.

I hurried past Mrs Lilac who was in the process of trying to persuade Connor

Mitchell, the most **embarrassed** boy in the school, to be in the play.

'Oh my darling Connor,' she cooed.

But of course! You are the Friar!
Friar Lawrence! That stage presence,
wonderful diction, air of authority!
Come, come, Connor my darling,
seize the day! Grasp the nettle!
Auditions are starting soon!

-8-

Wherefore Art I, Juliet?

At the auditions, Mrs Lilac was VERY impressed with Sonja *and* Myf's auditions for the part of Juliet's nurse (even though Myf was reading it very badly and Sonja was shouting her lines in a very threatening manner.

GOD YE GOOD
MORROW, GENTLEMEN
(OR ELSE).

She said they both had wonderful voice projection (very LOUD voices) and that she was in a quandary over who to choose.

Sonja suggested an arm wrestle to determine it.

Miss, that's not fair!

Ooh, well, it does seem a bit –
It's fine by me!

Myf was SO determined and put up such a good fight that she managed to hold off Sonja's victory for twenty minutes by keeping her hand 1mm off the table.

Then it was the auditions for the parts of Romeo and Juliet. Mrs Lilac said Sandy should audition with Cicily and that I should audition with Roger. I tried not to mind – after all, I had a crush on Roger again now so it was *fitting* that we should audition together.

We all sat in a row and watched Cicily and Sandy. Cicily was completely nauseating! She was dressed in an Elizabethan get-up and had learnt the part inside out, and was doing all these embarrassing theatrical gestures and talking in a silly actressy voice. I had to admit that Sandy made quite a good Romeo . . . he managed to say the lines so you could understand what he was saying – more or less – and sounded quite natural.

At the end, the LOUD tutting at Cicily from the row of other kids waiting to audition was drowned out by Mrs Lilac's clapping and cheering.

Now it was my turn, and I got up to follow Roger onstage.

Out of the corner of my eye I could see Sandy smiling up at me as I walked past him.

'Break a leg, Jelly!' he said.

'What?' I said, and immediately tripped over a brick that had appeared from nowhere.

'Are you OK, Jelly darling?' Mrs Lilac cried.

'Yes, I'm fine,' I whimpered, even though I definitely wasn't fine, and was completely **embarrassed** to have fallen over in front of Sandy.

My foot was *really* throbbing but I was determined to do my audition. I limped up to the stage, but couldn't really stand properly so Mrs Lilac suggested I do it sitting on a chair. It was HOPELESS! I was

supposed to be dancing about at a masked ball!

And Roger didn't help. He kept reading out Juliet's lines and treading on my foot.

Our audition was a bit like this . . .

Wherefore art thou, Romeo?
No! Wherefore art thou, Romeo?
Ow!

I was in agony, but because I had an audience I refrained from screaming blue murder.

As soon as it was over, I hopped back to my seat (my foot felt like a jellyfish sting dangling from my leg).

When I got back in my seat, Roobs said, 'Are you all right, Jelly?'

And Myf said, 'Sandy told you to

break your leg – he's a pig!'

Mrs Lilac came over to see if I was all right. I told her I was because I just wanted her to go away so I could screeeaaaaaam.

'Jelly darling, that was a VERY interesting audition . . . and, Roger, the way you kept echoing Juliet's lines was very original . . . But I really have no choice but to cast Sandy and Cicily as my star-crossed lovers!'

'Fine,' I said (I didn't care – I just wanted everyone to GO!!!).

Cicily was jumping up and down with glee but Sandy left her and came over to me,

'Is your foot all right, Jelly?'

'Yes, thanks,' I said, a bit rudely because I just wanted to be ALONE!

Then I saw that Cicily's mum had come to collect her and I could hear Cicily saying:

'Mummy! Is it OK if Sandy comes back to ours? We really should start rehearsing straight away!'

'Oh, I can't, Mrs Fanshaw, thank you. I've got a band rehearsal.'

And then as Mrs Fanshaw went to pick up Cicily's bag of clothes and make-up she said:

Don't be silly, Sandy! You must come. I've made Elizabethan hog pie especially. Come, come!

'I . . . er . . .' Sandy said.

'And could you carry Cicily's bag, Sandy dear?'

Sandy sighed and went over to help. 'Certainly, Mrs Fanshaw,' he said politely.

Mrs Fanshaw said to Cicily: 'What *have* you got in there, darling? A ton of bricks?'

Sandy turned and gave me a SIGNIFICANT LOOK (that I didn't understand) and then lugged Cicily's bag out of the school hall.

Bricks . . . bricks . . . ? I had tripped over a brick that had appeared from nowhere, hadn't I?! And I suddenly remembered – Cicily's dad was a bricklayer! She would stop at NOTHING to get what she wanted!!

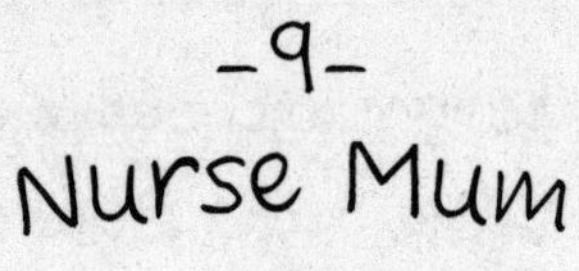

– 9 –
Nurse Mum

I was annoyed that Sandy had gone off with Cicily, even though he was probably just being polite. Sometimes you can be TOO polite. I started slowly putting my things in my bag as I waited for everyone to drift off.

Mrs Lilac was the last one to leave.

'Bye-bye, girls!'

As soon as the door swung closed behind her and her footsteps disappeared . . .

Waah aaah! My foo-oo-ooot!
Hurry up, Jelly! We're going to miss the bus!
Swelling up nicely

I told them to go without me because I couldn't rush, and being loyal and patient friends – they went without me! Then Roger suddenly reappeared, having forgotten his bag.

Just go without me! Waaah!
Are you all right, Jelly?

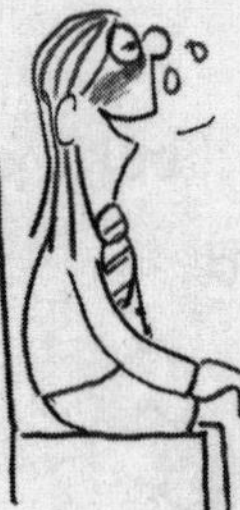

I'm fine thanks, Roger.
(Blushing when you are white as a sheet is no mean feat.)

Roger insisted on waiting for the next bus with me and getting me home safely. He was so kind – unlike Sandy the Polite Pig – and so handsome too. I definitely,

definitely had a crush on Roger again and had totally forgotten about Sandy and Cicily.

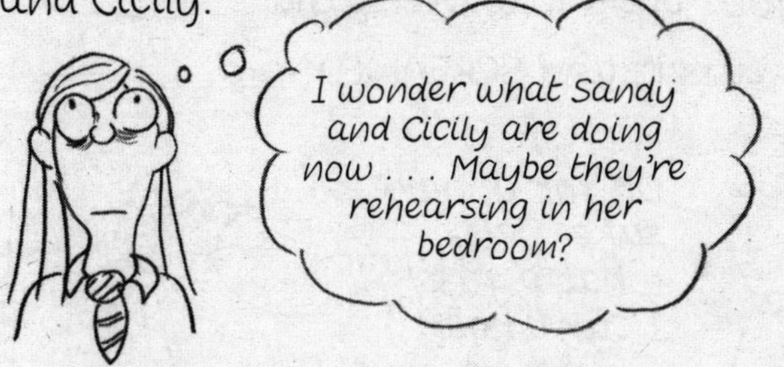

I wonder what Sandy and Cicily are doing now . . . Maybe they're rehearsing in her bedroom?

When I told my family that I thought I'd broken my foot they reacted like this:

Stop showing off, Jelly.
You've always had a low pain threshold.
Poor Jelly . . .

Julian tried to put a bag of frozen peas on my foot but I couldn't stand the weight of it.

Then he found a frozen bay leaf and tried to put that on my foot but I couldn't stand that either, and SCREAMED.

Oh for goodness sake, Jelly, what a fuss! I can't hear my programme!

Mum would make an appalling nurse.

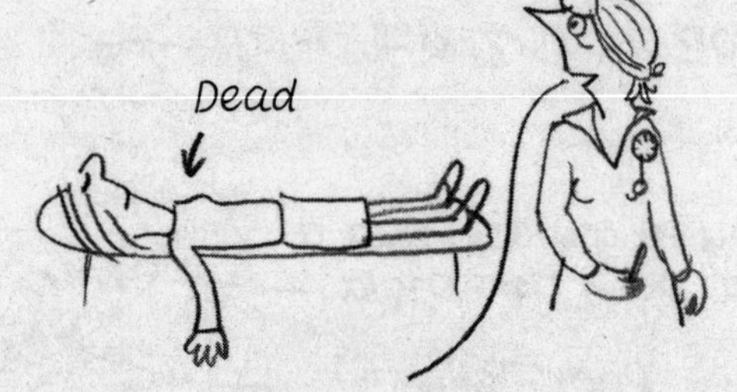

Honestly, Mrs Harris! What a fuss! You're not dead – you're probably just asleep!

-10-

Hammy Roles

The next day the pain had subsided but the disappointment about not getting a part in the play hadn't. However, Roobs had a suggestion:

'Why don't we sign up to do the catering? Then at least we can all go to the after-play party!'

So we did, and Mrs Lilac said that as we were going to be at all the rehearsals Myf and I should be understudies for Cicily and Sonja. She said that we were such wonderful, sensitive actresses with incredible stage presence! She also made Roger understudy for Romeo. I'm not sure he knew what that meant, but he did look very handsome.

She gave us all copies of the play and

told us to learn our parts thoroughly *just in case*. There was NO chance I would ever have to understudy for Cicily – she would **NEVER** be ill. Myf, however, thought there was a strong chance Sonja might be ill.

'She looks the sickly type,' she said. 'I'm going to learn my part.'

OK, Clever Clogs, what's your first line?

Oh . . . forsooth something or other? Don't worry – I'll remember if I have to go on.

Our job as caterers during rehearsals for *Romeo and Juliet* was to provide refreshments during breaks.

'What wonderful squash!' Mrs Lilac exclaimed. 'What delicious ham rolls! And yummy bickies! Did you make them? No? So beeeautifully chosen then. Perfect!'

We also had to concentrate on the play because of mine and Myf's important roles as understudies:

The only thing that *occasionally* kept us awake during rehearsals was Connor Mitchell who had been flattered/persuaded/hypnotised/bribed into playing the part of Friar Lawrence (whoever *he* was) – partly because no one else had auditioned.

During a scene with Juliet and

Friar Lawrence, Cicily gave a lively (if nauseating) performance as Juliet, but Connor – despite Mrs Lilac's protestations of his stage presence, natural good lOOKs, depth of voice – and that he was the new Johnny Depp – was so monotone and Stiff that it was funny.

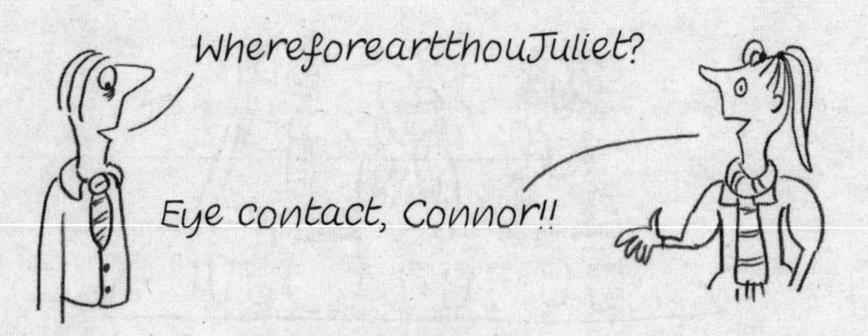

WhereforeartthouJuliet?
Eye contact, Connor!!

Miss! The caterers are laughing – it's very off-putting.
Oh, Cicily darling, I'm sure it's just the excitement and drama of the play that's filling them with joy and high spirits.

And because Sandy missed the first few rehearsals due to 'band commitments' (pig), Roger was having to understudy for Romeo, which Myf and Roobs also found hilarious because he still got muddled up and said Juliet's lines. But I was loyal to Roger and didn't laugh – and I did actually think his acting was quite ~~handsome~~ good.

And *obviously* NONE of us laughed or fell asleep when Sonja Perkins was on playing the Nurse. We didn't want to be challenged to an arm wrestle. Myf still couldn't raise her arm higher than her shoulder from holding her off for twenty minutes.

SEEK HAPPY NIGHTS TO HAPPY DAYS (or else).
Rubbish! I'd be MUCH better!

–11–
Dog's Got Talent

When I got home I decided to make myself five pieces of toast because no one seemed to be around to tell me not to. Suddenly, I heard a weird noise and then Fatty going mad barking upstairs – which meant there was almost definitely an intruder. So I went to investigate with Jay's baseball bat.

As I walked into their bedroom, Mum and Julian were sitting on the bed 'singing'!

Daddy was a milkman
workin' days and nights . . .
aah
ooh

Deliverin' the white stuff
and gettin' into fights . . .

Hi, Jelly! Guess what!? We've formed a folk duo – Sue 'n' Julian – and we're entering Boxford's Got Talent like you!

You can't enter Boxford's Got Talent!

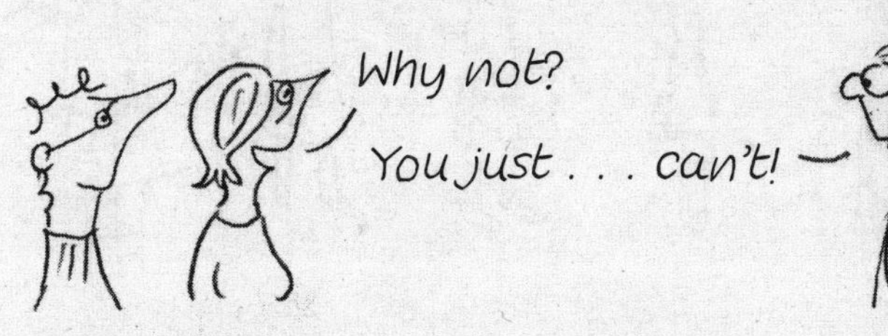

She's right, Sue.

Shut up, Julian. Give me one good reason, Jelly?

Where do I start? Too old, too embarrassing, can't play, can't sing . . .

Anyway <u>YOU</u> can't sing!

Finally she admits it! After years of me singing in front of her and waiting for a compliment.

La, la la.
La, la la.
La, la la.
Laaaah!

Sue 'n' Julian soon got two new members for their band and there wasn't a lot they could do about it.

Julian has been learning the violin for six years and hasn't got any better. Mum usually makes him go to the shed (*my* shed and the headquarters of The Faithful Club) when he gets the urge to make a horrific screeching noise.

But he does have one major fan – Cat. Cat has a BIG THING for Julian's violin 'music'. She leaps on to his shoulder and crawls along his arm, whereupon she languishes in ecstasy, occasionally letting out a l o n g yowl (which could possibly, if you were tone deaf, be said to be in harmony).

Fatty always liked to sing along when I played the recorder . . .

And Mum's screechy folk voice seems to get him going in **EXACTLY** the same way.

So NOW their band has become 'Sue, Julian, Cat 'n' Fats's Folk Combo'. Mum seems to think that the novelty element of having animals in their act might help them **WIN**. She keeps going on about that dog who won *Britain's Got Dogs*. Not DOGS, I tell her. 'TALENT'. It has to be someone *TALENTED* – *especially* if it is a dog.

Fatty barked at me quite aggressively.

'Yes, OK, you've got a modicum of talent,' I told Fatty, 'but just not ENOUGH – any of you!'

I was so **embarrassed** about Mum, Julian, Cat 'n' Fats's Folk Combo entering Boxford's Got Talent that I actually went off and read the Terms and Conditions of the competition that no one EVER reads. They just tick the box that says they've read it without any feeling of guilt.

Well, I read it!! It took me two hours and a large magnifying glass to wade through it. I think I should win a prize – say, 'Best Solo Artist Who Has Read the Terms and

Conditions' – just for reading it.

Sadly, there is absolutely NOTHING in there about age limits or animals. So animals, old people and even old animals can enter!!! It's OUTRAGEOUS!!

-12-
Back-stabbing Singers

The next rehearsal for Romeo and Juliet was the first one Sandy was able to come to. Myf, Roobs and I were just setting out the refreshments when he turned up. He looked like he was coming over to say hello but then Cicily approached with a clipboard.

Romeo! Why for art thou late?
Cicily's scarf
My scarf?

She was immersing herself in the part, which meant wearing Elizabethan clothes outside school (except for Sandy's scarf which was tied tightly round her scrawny neck), staying in character until the opening of the play . . . and obsessing about ~~Sandy~~ Romeo. Annoyingly, Sandy still seemed to be wearing Cicily's scarf, but as I was only looking out of the corner of my eye I couldn't see whether he still had mine on underneath.

During their scenes together, I noticed that Sandy and Cicily seemed to be getting on quite well. They kept giggling, and at one point even started singing Rhianna's 'Romeo and Juliet'. Cicily was TOTALLY flat and tuneless. A bit like a young female fog horn.

However, Mrs Lilac, who **obviously** had rose-tinted ears as well as glasses said ....

How beeeaautiful! You sound like angels!

'Do you know,' she continued, 'I have an idea! Why don't we incorporate that song into the play? Update things a little. You could give it an Elizabethan flavour! Can you by any chance play the lute, Sandy darling?'

'Not at all,' Sandy said, looking nervous.

Myf's crush, Benji Butler, and the other members of sO.M.G.! were hanging about at the back of the hall because they had a band rehearsal afterwards and they **burst** out **LAUGHING** at this.

Ha, ha, ha . . .

Then at break time, while we were serving up squash and biscuits, I overheard Sandy and Cicily talking as they stood in the queue:

'We musteth stay entwined as mucheth as the gods alloweth, forsooth our love will seemeth real for the performance, Romeo,' Cicily said, hanging on to Sandy's arm.

'Er, righto,' Sandy said.

Then Benji came over, smirking.

I didn't know you could sing, Cicily.
Forsooth, they named me Juliet.
Oh, yes, sorry. You haveth a sweet voice, Juliet.

No she doesn't!

Myf shouted from the refreshments table.

'Thank you, kind sir!' Cicily chirruped, 'Wouldst thou alloweth me to joineth your travelling minstrels troupe to maketh song behindeth thou?'

'What?' Benji **LAUGHED**.

'I feelest thou needest more oomph in thine song.'

'Eh?'

'CAN MY FRIEND POLLY AND I BE BACKING SINGERS FOR sO.M.G.!??' she shouted.

'Er . . . well – I . . . suppose,' Benji blustered.

'Forsooth I sing like the lark with joy!!' Cicily cooed, before turning round and yelling to Polly at the back of the queue,

Oi, Poll! Benji says we can be backing singers for sO.M.G.!!

Polly Pearson was playing second maid to Cicily/Juliet, which was kind of how their

friendship worked in real life.

Myf nudged me. 'Did you hear that? Benji's letting Cicily be a backing singer in sO.M.G.!'

'Oh for Gawd's sake,' I muttered, 'we could have been backing singers for sO.M.G.!'

'But we can't sing,' Roobs reminded me.

'So?! Neither can they!'

Then we heard Benji saying: 'We should have three backing singers really,' and then to Sonja, 'Hey, Son, how about you do backing vocals for us too?'

He'd pulled one of her headphones away from her ear.

Oi! Do that again, Benji, and I'll whack you!

Benji wasn't *scared* of Sonja – he was fearless like Myf – which was why he and Myf had always got on so well.

He yanked Sonja's other headphone away from her other ear. 'Just thought you'd look COOL as one of our backing singers, that's all.'

And he went off laughing.

'Oh, now he's asking SONJA to be a backing singer!' I told Myf.

Myf looked outraged and shouted:

'WE DON'T WANT TO BE BACKING SINGERS, JELLY! WE'VE GOT OUR OWN BAND!'

–13–
Jellyous

As Cicily and Sandy got to the front of the queue Cicily said under her breath to me:

Jealous are you, Jelly?

Not in the slightest.

'So what's your band called, Jelly?' Sandy asked.

'Jelly and the Mould Breakers,' I muttered, busying myself with some rich tea biscuits.

'We're going to win Boxford's Got Talent,' Myf informed him.

'You've entered! Brilliant!' said Sandy.

'Why dost thou and sO.M.G.! not entereth Boxford Hath Talent, Romeo?' Cicily asked Sandy.

'We're only a covers band – we just sing O.M.G.! songs.'

'WE are a . . .' Roobs got out her clipboard and read out,

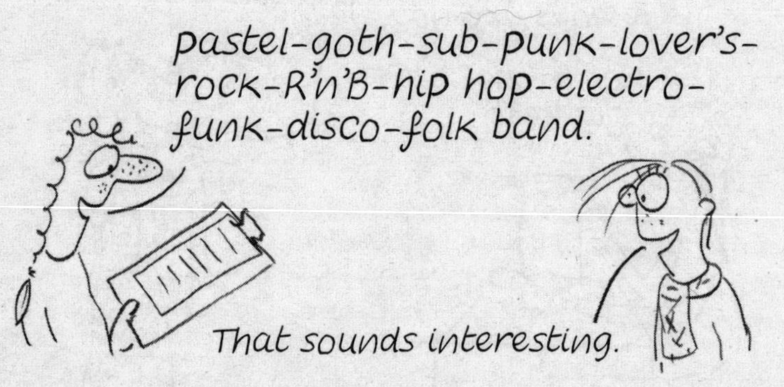

pastel-goth-sub-punk-lover's-rock-R'n'B-hip hop-electro-funk-disco-folk band.
That sounds interesting.

'How totally stupid!!' Cicily said, forgetting to be Elizabethan.

'So when can I come and hear you play?' Sandy said, ignoring Cicily.

The word 'play' made me **blush** even more as we still hadn't learnt any instruments or written any songs.

'Well,' I said to the rich tea biscuit I was arranging on a plate,

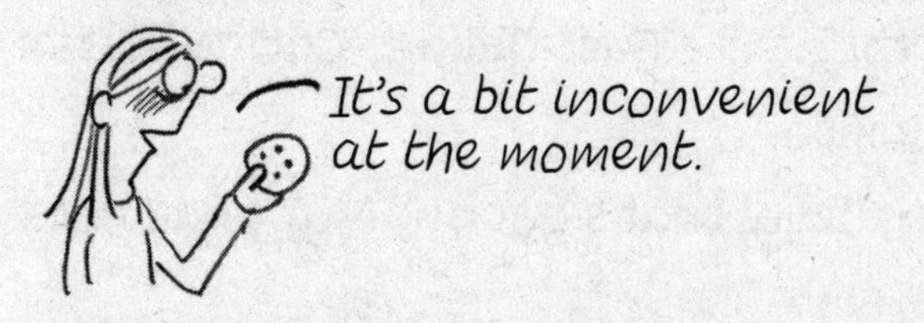
It's a bit inconvenient at the moment.

'Anyway, Romeo, you haven't got time for that with all your gigs and your major role in a Shakespearean production,' Cicily squawked.

'Well, I'm sure I could fit in going to see Jelly and the Mould Breakers,' Sandy smiled.

'And anyway,' Cicily continued (now completely speaking in Elizabethan-the-second-ish), 'I've heard there's a dead cert for the winner of Boxford's Got Talent this year – apparently Silas Crowe really likes animal acts *and* he's judging the over twenty-fives.'

I felt my chest melting into my knees. I knew exactly what she was going to say, but I still hoped she wouldn't . . .

'My uncle's a bookie and he said the odds are on . . .' (long pause like on *The X Factor*) '. . . Sue, Julian, Cat 'n' Fats's Folk Combo.'

'Hey, Jelly, that's your—' Myf and Roobs began.

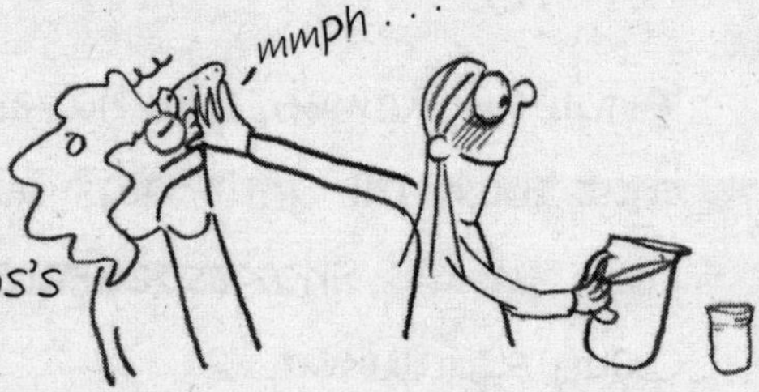

I put my hands over Myf's and Roobs's mouths, which made it quite hard to serve squash.

'Apparently they're rubbish,' Cicily prattled on, 'but Silas Crowe loves dogs, cats and older people.'

'Hold on,' Sandy interrupted. 'Jelly? Isn't your mum called Sue, your stepdad called Julian, your cat called Cat . . . and your dog's called Fatty, isn't he?'

I was slightly flattered that he remembered so much about my family, but of course I had to deny everything.

'Ha ha ha! Not at all!' I said as though

the very idea was utterly ridiculous. 'I don't know ANYONE called Sue, Julian, Fatty OR Cat.'

Then Cicily dragged him away.

C'mon, Sandy, we've got a band rehearsal to go to.

And as they went off I heard her say: 'And there's this REEEAAALLY old woman who's entered – she's got a good chance too because she wears a FOX STOLE apparently, which is a *sort* of animal, and she's way way WAY over twenty-five – Carol or Garol? Grannie? Sings the blues or something . . .'

Sandy glanced back at me (he'd met my granny, Grarol, when **sO.M.G.!** played at my mum's wedding) and I made sure I was doing **LOUD** laughing with Roger who had just asked how the bass playing was going.

'What's funny, Jelly?' Roger asked, in his dim-yet-handsome way, although it was a perfectly intelligent question in this instance.

'She hasn't even picked it up, Roger!!' Myf shouted. 'But she's laughing cos her granny's entered Boxford's Got Talent!!'

'ShuddUP, Myf!' I growled.

My granny isn't called 'Granny'. Instead, we call her 'Grarol' because when Jay and I were little she wasn't sure about being called Granny (especially when there were attractive men around). So she insisted we called her Carol (her name) – but we'd forget and go to say 'Gra–' then see her alarmed expression and quickly try to change it to Carol – so it became 'Gra-rol'.

Grarol wasn't completely sure about this new name, but at least it didn't make her sound old (just completely weird).

Good-looking man
Gra . . .
. . . rol?

–14–
It's Her Age

'Pleeeaaaase tell me it's not true,' I said to Mum when I got home.

'Look, Jelly, you'll just have to accept that Julian, Cat, Fatty and I are entering Boxford's Got Talent. We're not dead yet, you know.'

'Not that,' I told her. '*Grarol.*'

'Oh that! I'm afraid so. You know how competitive she is. She's upstairs getting dressed up. Don't challenge her – you know it's not worth it – uh-oh, here she comes . . .'

Presenting . . .

Grarol Sings the BLUES! (3/1 to win at Fanshaw's bookmakers!)

Grarol was one of those people who thought she was good at everything – and therefore by association any relative of hers was also good at everything (but not quite as good as her).

Can't you just be a
normal grandmother
and go to bingo or
something?
That's ageist
and sexist, Jelly!

I can't take
any more!

I stormed up to my room and waited for someone to follow me. Twenty minutes of snivelling later no one had appeared so I decided to do some **EXTRA-LOUD** crying.

I was also getting hungry and I could **smell** Julian's chicken curry cooking . . .

I heard Grarol say:

'It's her age.'

And Mum say:

'It's her hormones.'

And Grarol add:

'Yes, the combination can make you very angry.'

It's not my AGE and it's not my HORMONES and I'm NOT ANGRY!

I shouted angrily like a thirteen-year-old girl with raging hormones.

Mum poked her head round the door.

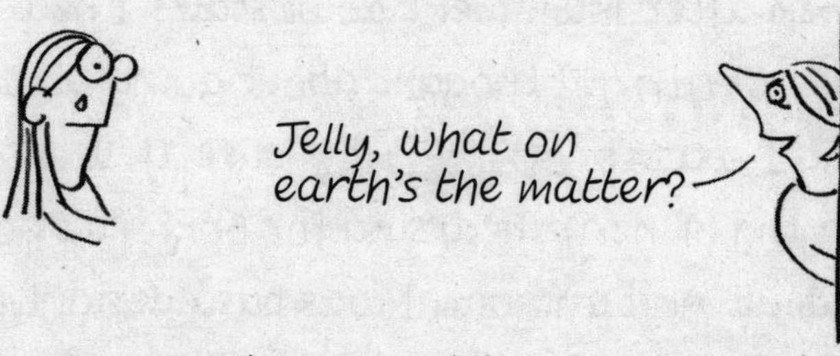

Jelly, what on earth's the matter?

she said, trying not to sound irritable.

I don't know! I don't want to be horrible, but it's very embarrassing having your family enter Boxford's Got Talent. (More blubbing.)

OK, Sue, Julian, Cat 'n' Fats won't enter this year. I don't want to cramp your style.

Julian heading upstairs.

Phew!

Really? What about Grarol?

Grarol I can do nothing about, I'm afraid.

Then after Mum went downstairs I heard <u>her</u> crying. I thought about going down but I wasn't **EXACTLY** sure if it was crying or her rehearsing for Boxford's Got Talent. And anyway I was busy designing a poster for Jelly and the Mould Breakers (Myf and Roobs were due round later).

But then it got VERY loud and I knew it had to be crying – SURELY ....??

What on earth's the matter, Mum?

I said, trying not to sound irritable.

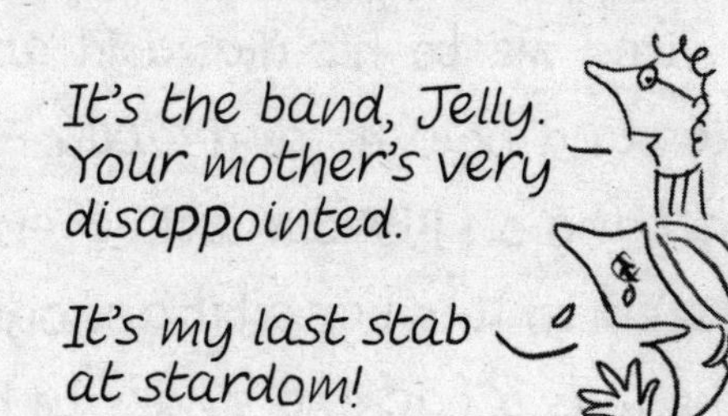

It's the band, Jelly. Your mother's very disappointed.
It's my last stab at stardom!

Oh God, whatever! I don't mind if you enter, if you really want to.
Really?
MIMING: For God's sake, no!

But you were SO upset – you were making that dreadful noise!!
I'm upset about something else.
Oh good! I mean . . . what is it, darling?

I explained to Mum and Julian that Sandy had invited me to his gig, and about the groupies and how he and Cicily Fanshaw were getting on **REALLY** well, even though he did seem to find her a **bit** annoying, and now she was a backing singer in his band as well, and she had stolen his scarf off me and I hadn't had a chance to explain that I didn't throw it away and NOW he was wearing *her* scarf and she was really confident and pushy and bossy but he still went off with her!

Julian cleared his throat.

Mum said: 'A lot of men – boys – like

to be bossed about and organised – don't they, Julian?'

'Er—'

'I mean, if I hadn't bossed and organised Julian he'd still be living in his bedsit playing his violin and eating takeaways . . .'

Julian had a faraway look in his eyes, and a little smile curling up the corners of his lips.

'. . . and he wouldn't be married to me,' Mum continued, 'cooking me lovely dinners and playing in an up-and-coming folk combo. Some men – boys – are not at all sure about themselves, or confident with girls or know what they want. So, if a bossy girl comes along and is all keen and says what *she* wants, sometimes they just go along with it. It's not just us girls who are shy and unsure, is it, Julian?'

'Not in the least,' Julian said, **winking** at me.

Mum lost her concentration then and started on about something else.

Julian said to me, 'Don't be too bossy, Jells. Don't tell your mother I said that though. Just be warm and friendly – that's all that's needed.'

Mum had managed to confuse me with her giant personality again. I didn't *know* what I wanted! And I didn't *want* to be bossy. I just felt very, very, very, very, very, VERY, VERY upset and that the WHOLE world was against me. That's all.

I felt so sorry for myself that I decided to cry into the mirror for a bit so I could really enjoy the full effect of my misery. It was a new three-way mirror Mum had got from Auntie Val.

And that's when 'IT' happened!! I saw my profile LIVE for the first time – and my ears in profile LIVE for the first time, more to the point.

Of course I'd seen my ears in photos – but that wasn't 'real life'. NOW I could see my living, breathing, *actual* Profile – and it was a terrible SHOCK!! I didn't recognise myself!

And my ears looked GINORMOUS again! I say *AGAIN* because I used to think I had big ears because Grarol used to say I looked like a little elephant and then I got over that and then years later Billy Rumble the school bully started calling me 'Dumbo' and I got all self-conscious about them again.

But then Sandy told me I had 'cute ears' last summer – and that compliment had lasted me all this time. But now I wasn't so sure – maybe he was just being **kind** when he said it? And anyway, with everything that had been going on, the effect of his compliment had started to wear off. The more I looked at my profile in the three-way mirror, the **BIGGER** my ears looked.

-16-

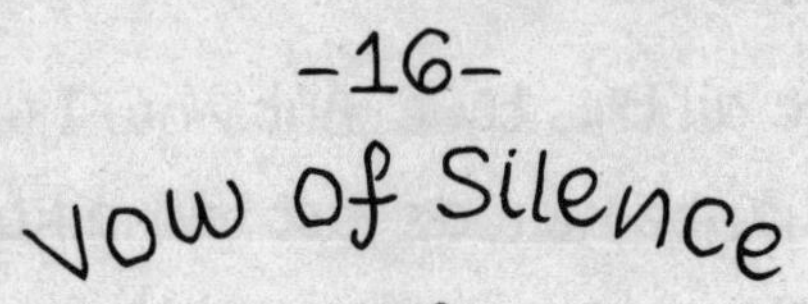

Myf, Roobs and I were having a jamming session. We had written a song – well, Myf had written some lyrics apparently and we were going to try to set them to music (must learn instruments!!).

I informed Myf and Roobs that I had discovered my ears in PROFILE and was only going to show my face front on from now on. I explained why – but they were ***totally*** uninterested.

Myf started to read out her lyrics. They needed some tweaks here and there, but for a THICKO she'd done quite well.

They went like this:

Love, love me please,
Don't be a tease,
I'll always be true,
So plee-ee-ee-ease,
Love me please.

She even had quite a good tune to go with it. We decided to record it on my phone.

Myf introduced us:

'And now, ladies and gentlemen, the amazing new band, **MYF AND THE MOULD BREAKERS**!!'

She really wouldn't give up! She was such an EGO-MANIAC!

'No,' I told her, '**JELLY** and the Mould Breakers!'

'Oh OK. Jelly and the Mould Breakers Feat. MyfZ.H!'

'Oi!' Roobs cried. 'Feat. RoobZ.M as well!'

'Oh all *right*,' Myf said. 'Jelly and the Mould Breakers (Feat. MyfZ.H (mainly) and RoobZ.M).'

Then the recording time on my phone ran out.

'Let's listen!' cried Myf (she's **SO** immature) 'It'll be a laugh!'

But Myf didn't laugh.

She had never heard her own speaking voice before except inside her own head.

Oh OK . . .

Please tell me I don't actually sound like that!

I sound like GARY HOOK!!

Gary Hook was a boy at our old junior school who was very brainy and had got

a scholarship to a posh school.
He had a squeaky yet nasally
voice.

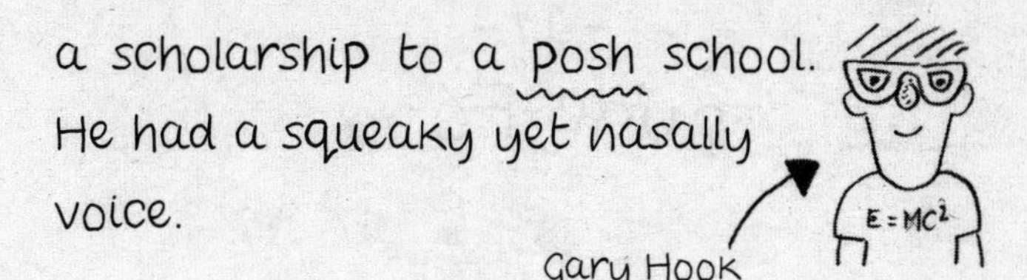

I'm never going to speak again!!

Roobs and I tried to LOOK sad.

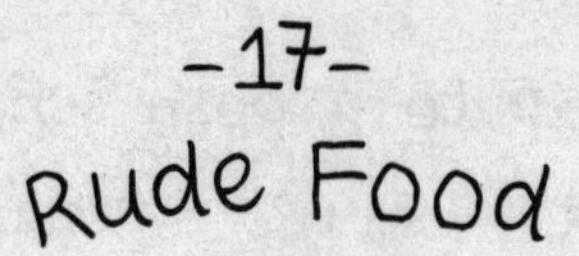

-17- Rude Food

The next night it was the dress rehearsal for the play (which is when everyone practises the play in full costume). We were lined up behind our catering table wearing the Jelly and the Mould Breakers T-shirts that we'd made. Myf was already TOTALLY over sounding like Gary Hook, which was unfortunate for me and Roobs as we'd quite enjoyed having a bit of peace and quiet.

Sonja is absolutely terrible as the nurse!!
She doesn't even know her lines!
JMB
JMB
JMB

(Still sounding like Gary Hook)

'How would you know, Gary?' I said.

Roobs and I laughed.

'Gary?' she asked.

'*Gary Hook*,' we reminded her.

'Who?'

'The one you sound like.'

'Sound like?'

(I told you she was over it – which in Myf's case means she's just forgotten all about it, which is the same thing if you think about it. Sadly, I hadn't forgotten about my profile.)

It was only a week till the *actual* performances of *Romeo and Juliet* and Roobs was getting very WORRIED about the catering. There were three performances of the play, two on the Saturday and one on the Sunday. As well as catering for the party on the Sunday we also had to do food on the Saturday between the matinee and the evening performance.

Roobs seems to have become what my mum calls a 'foodie' – which I think means giving silly or exotic-sounding names to perfectly ordinary food and then going on about it.

For example, food like sun-dried tomatoes . . . What they really are is dried tomatoes, which actually sounds quite yucky. Or wilted spinach which sounds even more yucky than spinach.

'Right,' said Roobs, clutching her notebook. 'I've studied the play and it has a lot of tragedy in it and is very sad so I want the food to be joyous and comforting to energise and calm the actors. How about for the catering between shows we do an *amuse bouche** like mini paninis?'

Myf and I giggled.

'What's so funny?'

* French for 'amuse mouth' – a tasty bite-sized bit of food for before or between meals.

'It sounds rude.' I told her.

'No, it <u>doesn't</u>, Myf! What about fajitas?'

we cried, spluttering with laughter. Myf guffawed so forcefully . . .

. . . she let out a very small fart of her own.

Then we both convulsed into giggles, and the more sternly Roobs looked at us the more we laughed.

Roobs sighed, 'What about quiche?'

Myf and I spluttered with more laughter even though it didn't sound at ALL rude.

'It's very easy,' Roobs continued. 'And we could give it a modern twist and lots of colour – for example, yellow and red peppers.'

Just then, Sonja came over looking like she was going to WHACK us. She had her Nurse's outfit on, but she didn't look very sympathetic (even less sympathetic than my mum looked when she was an imaginary nurse in my imagination).

Give us a drink and a biscuit.
← (Nurse outfit)

Roobs gave her some orange squash and a rich tea.

'Haven't you got a proper cup of tea? I like dunking my biscuits,' she snarled.

'Well,' Roobs began, going into foodie

mode, 'what you can do is dunk the rich tea in the orange squash for nine to ten seconds, then suck the juice out of it. Then, once softened, re-dunk for approximately three to four seconds, then eat. It has the same effect as hot tea but with a playful, summery orangey tang.'

Sonja stared at her. 'Shuddup, Rhubarb. Anyway, you lot, I fancy that Benji Butler, and I want to go out with him, so if you don't fix us up I'm going to whack you. Also, I want to be a backing singer in that SO.M.G.!, so fix that for me as well or I'll whack you again.'

I did a **BIG** sigh (which I thought was quite brave). Benji's flattery had ***obviously*** got him EVERYWHERE.

And Sonja went off over-dunking her rich tea biscuit so it fell in her squash. Myf looked outraged. She considered Benji Butler to be her boyfriend – even though all they ever did was bicker and laugh at each other.

I hate that Sonja. First she steals my part as the Nurse, and now she wants to steal my sort of boyfriend, and be a backing singer in SO.M.G.!

And I said:

I hate Cicily too. First she steals my part as Juliet, then she steals my sort of boyfriend and now she is a backing singer in SO.M.G.!

And Roobs, the voice of reason, said:

Woman up, for goodness sake, you two! You sound like a pair of fish husbands. We don't want to be backing singers, do we? We want to be the ACTUAL BAND!

–18–
In the Soup

On Saturday, Roobs, Myf and I got to the school hall early to start preparing the meal for the cast and crew. There was only an hour between the matinee and the evening performance, so there wasn't enough time for everyone to go home to eat. It was our job to feed them all.

While everyone was preparing to go on for the first performance we were sweating and slaving in the kitchen. We were feeling very left out. Cicily was being very annoying and making everyone stand in a BIG circle and do breathing exercises and Sandy hadn't glanced towards the kitchen once.

Myf and I were being bossed about by Roobs who was making us call her 'Chef' and treating us like we were on Master Chef (the Complete Amateurs).

This was Roobs's menu for the meal:

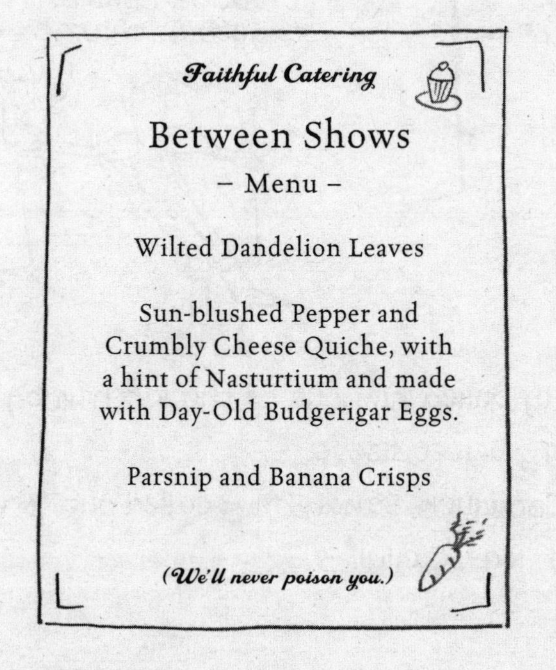

Faithful Catering

Between Shows

– Menu –

Wilted Dandelion Leaves

Sun-blushed Pepper and Crumbly Cheese Quiche, with a hint of Nasturtium and made with Day-Old Budgerigar Eggs.

Parsnip and Banana Crisps

(We'll never poison you.)

Sandy popped his head round the door. I couldn't help noticing that, for a pig, he looked quite attractive in a pair of tights.

Hello, Myf, Roobs. Hi, Jelly. Smells delicious. See you after the matinee . . . I—

Forsooth, Romeo, stayeth in character!

Cicily pulled him out of the kitchen by his puffy velvet sleeve.

'Good luck, Sandy!' Myf called out. 'Break both legs, Cicily!'

Everyone was very NERVOUS before going on and there was quite a big queue of people for the loo, clutching their stomachs.

Even Cicily was looking green about the gills, and she NEVER got nervous. But the play obviously went well because there was rapturous applause at the interval (annoyingly).

Roobs was shouting about the carrot soup. 'Come on, you two – get those carrots chopped and in the blender!'

'My hand's aching!' Myf cried.

'Mine too!'

'One minute left!' Roobs yelled.

'Come on,' Myf whispered. 'Let's just put the carrots in whole, what difference does it make? . . . Yes, Chef!'

'And don't get any leaves in there – they're poisonous!'

'We might have got a few leaves in there, Chef . . . !' I told her.

'A few won't matter. It's only poisonous if you eat loads and loads. Right, soup in the vat and on table – ten seconds till serving!'

'Yes, Chef!'

We heard the even more annoyingly rapturous applause after the final scene of the play and everyone came through to the kitchen laughing and clattering and calling each other 'darling'.

Myf whispered to me, 'We actually did put a LOT of those leaves in the soup – it might be really poisonous – poisonous enough to make certain people a bit poorly if we give them enough . . .'

We decided we were going to give tiny portions to the people we liked, and bigger portions to the people who we didn't like.

Sandy was first in the queue.

Ooh, carrot soup! My favourite.
I'm famished! Big portion, please!

Which was slightly awkward as I did like him even though he was a pig. But luckily

Sandy was a very gentlemanly pig and when Cicily came skipping over – 'Romeo! I too am famished!' – he let her in front.

Myf gave Cicily a ginormous bowl of soup but there was still quite a lot left for Sandy.

Luckily Sonja was very un-gentle-womanly and shoved herself in front of Sandy.

'Soup, please, and make it a big one else I'll whack you.'

More – more – more – more –
Have as much as you like, Sonja!

On the other side of the kitchen I could see Cicily feeding Sandy spoonfuls of soup in a **very** cosy way.

When Sandy caught my eye, I couldn't turn away (ears) so continued to stare until HE looked away. See! **Ashamed**! He was ashamed because he had forsaken me for another girl.

Myf and I left Roobs to load the dishwasher because she didn't like the way we did it at *all* – so to get out of it we'd started laying the cutlery horizontally on top of the cutlery section and putting the plates in with three-quarters of a nourishing meal left on them.

Oh I'll do it!!!! Honestly, if you want something done properly – do it yourself!

-19-
Murdering the Play

Myf and I snuck off to watch the second half of the evening performance from the wings – neither of us had watched it properly before because we were either too busy napping or making badges for Jelly and the Mould Breakers and we hadn't bothered learning our parts (what would be the POINT?? We knew Sonja and Cicily would never give us the chance to be understudies!).

But as there was NOW a possibility that our soup **might** make them poorly and unable to go on the next day we thought we'd better try to concentrate. But it was quite confusing with all the funny language and after ten minutes or so we both nodded off.

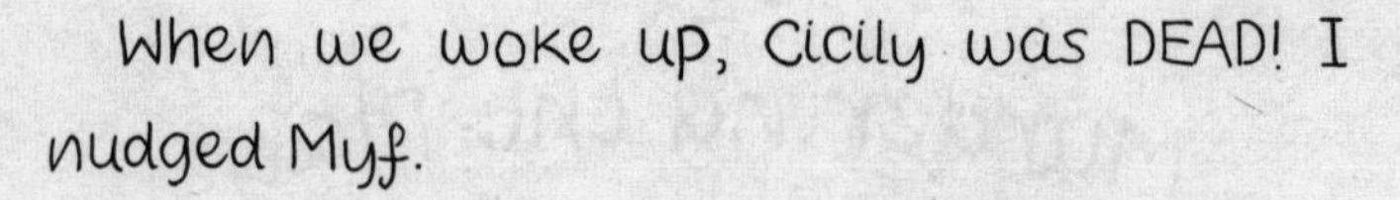
When we woke up, Cicily was DEAD! I nudged Myf.

Look at Cicily! She's dead! Sandy just said so! We've poisoned her!
Oh my love, my wife! Death!

Have we poisoned Sonja too?
Don't you understand? We've M-U-R-D-E-R-E-D Cicily!!
Look! She's completely dead!
Oh dear.

Despite the fact that my blood was running **COLD** with fear I still noticed that Sandy seemed to be *very* distraught about Cicily's death.

'We'll have to make a run for it and hide out somewhere!' I told Myf.

We ran to the kitchen to get Roobs. But she wasn't there! She'd left a note saying she'd gone to purchase dishwasher salt – so I turned the note over and left *her* a note:

Cicily's dead!
We are hiding in
sports cupboard
waiting for
cover
of darkness.
See you there.

X

It was very uncomfortable in the cupboard – and very **smelly**.

Myf said, 'I wonder if Sonja is dead yet?'

'Myf! You don't seem to get it – we have MURDERED Cicily!!'

'What? In real life?'

'Yes! With the carrot leaves! In the soup!'

'Can you leave fingerprints on soup?' Myf asked.

'We'll have to go to prison for the rest of our lives!' I cried.

'But what about Myf and the Mould Breakers?' Myf whined.

'JELLY and the Mould Breakers, for crying out loud!!'

'And Boxford's Got Talent?'

'Well, we won't be on trial by then so it should be . . . MYF!!! You don't understand the seriousness of it!! And can you paleeease get your elbow out of my ear!'

We're going to have to run away and start a new life!
Ooh, what about Gibraltar?

'Nah,' I said dismissively (I wasn't sure where it was). 'How about Scotland? My mum always says she's going to run away there when she's got P.M.T.'

'Too cold,' Myf said. 'What about China? We could get jobs in a trainers factory as child slaves.'

After much debate we eventually decided on Cornwall because we knew where it was, and thought we could start new lives as surfing instructors.

We would wait till the school was closed then walk to the coach station.

Then, despite the fact that I was sitting on a cricket stump (the pointy end up) and Myf was perched on a rugby ball (the pointy end up), we both nodded off for a bit.

–20–

Cupboard Love

Suddenly, we were woken by banging on the door.

'Myf? Jelly?'

It was Roobs.

'They're not here . . .' Myf croaked. 'Only Gary Hook is in here. That's me, Gary Hook.'

Then she continued to be Gary Hook in a voice that was more like Gary Hook than even Gary Hook's.

Hello, Roobs, how are you? – I haven't seen you since junior school . . .

'Myf, open up!' Roobs demanded.

We opened the door.

'What are you doing?' Roobs enquired.

We explained that we had poisoned at **LEAST** Cicily and possibly Sonja – if not the WHOLE cast – and that we were running away and starting a *new* life as surfing instructors in Cornwall.

'Don't be so utterly ridiculous!' Roobs said. 'You can't even surf! And anyway you haven't poisoned anyone – some of the cast have gone down with a 24-hour stomach bug that's been going round at school – although there have been unfair rumours that it was MY catering . . .'

'Oh . . .' Myf said, sounding a bit disappointed.

Has Sonja got it?

'Yes,' Roobs told her, helping her off the rugby ball, 'and Cicily and Sandy, and a few others. They don't think they'll be able to do the performance tomorrow. Mrs Lilac asked me to come and find you—'

'Phew! That's a relief,' I said, but then it dawned on me what that meant. We *were* going to have to go on as understudies! The **NEXT DAY!**

Roobs had studied the play in GREAT depth when planning her menu and explained that in the play Juliet takes a potion to make her look dead so she doesn't have to marry her fiancé, Paris, and can then run away with Romeo. But Romeo thinks she really IS dead and takes poison and *does* die, so then Juliet wakes up from her sleep and finds Romeo dead next to an empty bottle of poison. Juliet **kisses** Romeo to try to get some of the poison on her lips, but it doesn't work so she stabs herself.

'I see,' Myf said, not listening. I wasn't listening either, until Roobs got to the bit with 'kisses' in it . . . I felt panic rising in my chest. **Roger Lovely** would be going on as Romeo!

I flushed.

I was actually going to have to **Kiss** **Roger Lovely**.

-21-

I asked Myf to stay the night at mine so we could try to learn our lines. Feeling sick with NERVES I set about trying to quickly learn the part of Juliet. Myf still seemed to think she knew her lines for the part of the Nurse and said she would test me . . .

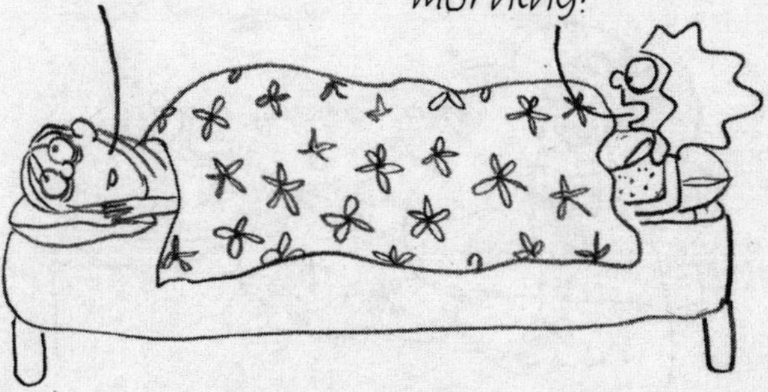

Um . . . dost thou?
Oh, what is it!?
Shut up, Jelly, it's four o'clock in the morning!

When I did finally get to sleep I had terrible dreams about being onstage in my underwear and not being able to remember my lines. I was so relieved to wake up and find it had all been a **BAD** dream, until I remembered it wasn't a bad dream – I really COULDN'T remember any of my lines!

Myf, however, was sleeping like a baby –

And the Oscar for best actress goes to . . . Myf Hughes!

And thanks to all my friends and family back in Boxford – losers!!!!

On the bus on the way to school I tried to learn my part again but the words were just swimming about on the page.

I can't remember my lines – I feel sick – really, really sick. I feel like I'm going to throw up and do diarrhoea.

Just relax! I'm not at all nervous!

Well you SHOULD be!

It was no good – I couldn't learn it! When we got to the hall Mrs Lilac said that it would be OK if I read from the page and she didn't look in the slightest bit annoyed – though she didn't *exactly* look happy, either.

Ten minutes before I had to go onstage I was still feeling very sick . . .

. . . but Myf was bouncing about with excitement in her giant Nurse's uniform.

-22-

Myf Shakespeare

My first scene with Roger was a disaster. As soon as he walked on all the girls in the audience started whistling and whooping and shouting, 'Phwoar!' He had to wear Sandy's costume, and Sandy's tights were a tad too small for him. He was reading from the script, too, but he kept reading out **MY** lines again so we got all confused. But no one could hear anyway because of all the whistling and whooping.

When it came to the first scene with Myf and me, Myf just made her lines up – total gobbledegook. I read out the right lines and she just said whatever she liked back.

'I don't think you should bother with that Romeo – he's a right creep.'

'For crying out loud, Juliet, you don't half go on!'

And such like.

But no one seemed to notice! (Though Mrs Lilac almost had the slightest, faintest, spidery frown line appearing in amongst her Smiley face.)

Stop making your lines up!
Why should I? I think they're better than Shakespeare's.

When it came to the bit where Friar Lawrence (Connor– shrieks of laughter from the audience) has given Juliet (me) the sleeping draught to make her seem dead –

I pretended to drink from the bottle and just lay down and looked as dead as possible.

But Myf ran on to the stage and started shaking me . . . .

Jelly – et!
Jelly – et!!
Wake up!!!!
Oh God, she SAID she was feeling really sick and that she thought she was going to do DIARRHOEA!
Why didn't I listen?!

'Oh no!!' she cried, picking up the plastic bleach bottle that the prop designer had dressed up to look like a bottle of sleeping draught. 'She's drunk this cleaning fluid – it's got a skull and crossbones on and it says "POISON – do not drink"!!'

Well I *wasn't* feeling very well but I wasn't dead and it was very hard to stay looking dead with Myf trying to give me the **kiss** of life. And **very** hard not to be sick. Then she threw herself on top of me and started wailing.

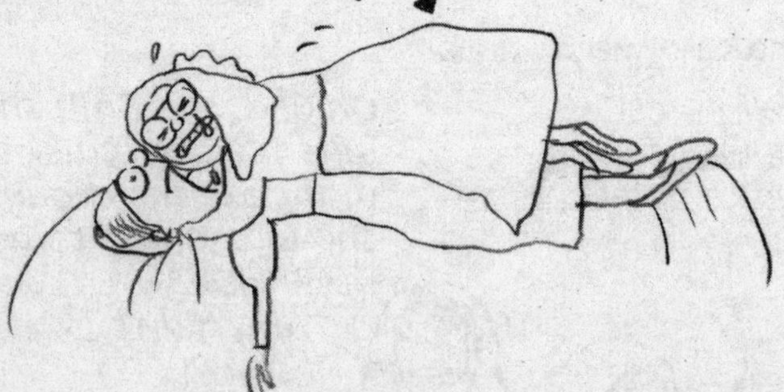

Connor quickly pulled the curtains across, and despite the **huge** applause for Myf's performance, Mrs Lilac's patience was now being a tiny bit tested. She explained to the hysterical Nurse Myf that she wasn't exactly *in* that scene and that I was only pretending to be dead.

She told me to reassure Myf that I was OK and I said I actually wasn't OK – I felt VERY SICK . . .

-23-
Sick at Heart

So the curtains opened on me lying 'dead' again for Romeo's entrance to the tomb. Roger stalked on to the stage to more whoops and whistles from the audience. He drank his vial of poison and dropped down 'dead' (his **Stiff** acting came in very handy in this scene).

Then I had to wake up and read out a lot of stuff and then it was time to **Kiss** him. I leant down towards him and suddenly retched and was **SICK**! It mostly went on the floor, but some went on Roger's hair

(I would've turned away but I was still feeling self-conscious about my ears).

'Urgh!' Roger exclaimed and jumped up. Mrs Lilac ran on with a bucket of water and mopped up the sick and gave me a wet wipe to clean my face.

The audience was quite getting into this new version of *Romeo and Juliet* and started cheering about Romeo being alive after all. So to put the story back on track I gave him the vial of 'poison' to drink and whispered to him to lie down and be dead again.

Then the audience started booing and shouting, 'Murderer!' So thinking better of trying to **kiss** him again, I stabbed myself and the audience cheered . . .

. . . which was quite upsetting when I'd been so poorly.

The curtains started to come across but Roger sat up before they met, wiping at his hair with his sleeve.

Seeing their hero alive once more, the audience started cheering again and the curtains closed to more rapturous applause.

'You've been SICK in my hair!' Roger exclaimed, turning to face me. He sounded a bit annoyed.

'Sorreee – urgh!' I retched again 'Ooh. Sorry, Roger.'

'It's all right,' he said, looking actually quite furious.

I followed him to the bathroom saying sorry a few more times. He got out his wash bag (which was ENORMOUS and full of all sorts of products: hair gel, hair wax, moisturiser, foundation, toner, concealer) and started dabbing and daubing at himself.

'Oh, I'll have to wash it now!' he said crossly. 'It took me ages to get it just right earlier.'

I thought I'd better leave him to it, and give him a chance to calm down, so I backed off.

–24–

Sonja the Second

Sonja reappeared then, having recovered from her stomach bug in time to see Myf getting praise for her *interesting* interpretation of the Nurse. She was LIVID, and had just pinned Myf to the wall and was threatening to whack her when someone threatened to whack HER.

It was a GIANT older version of Sonja. She even had the headphones and the LOUD voice.

You little fibber. You wosen in no play an it woz rubbish an' all.

Then, giant older Sonja went stomping off. Mrs Lilac came and put her arm round Sonja and even Sonja didn't have the heart to shrug her off, though she did say to us:

What you looking at, Titch! An' you, Dumbo, an' you, Rhubarb!

'Don't . . . !' Myf said to me and Roobs.

'I'm not going to!'

'Don't you dare!'

'I'm not!' said Roobs.

'If you start feeling sorry for Sonja, I'm never speaking to you again.'

'But, Myf, she had tears in her eyes.'

'And that sister of hers . . . Poor Sonja.'

'Shut up you three or else!!' Sonja yelled from the other side of the room.

Then Mum turned up, saying: 'That poor girl.'

'Yes,' Julian agreed from behind her. 'School bullies are often being bullied elsewhere, usually at home.'

'She's still a bully!' Myf said, looking over and seeing Sonja laughing with Benji Butler.

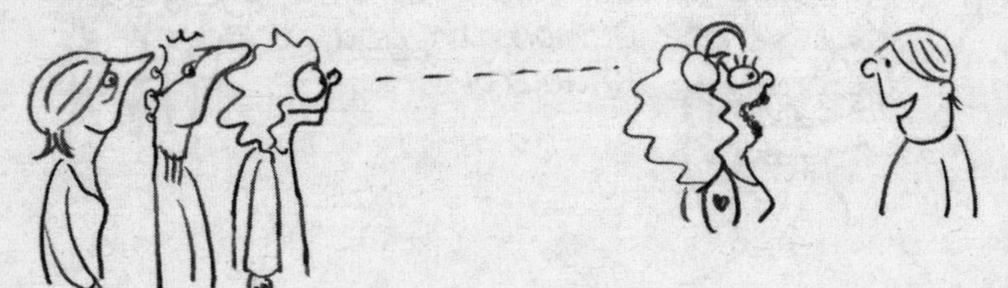

-25-
Stare Out

Although I was still feeling a bit ill, I managed to get to the after-play party. Everyone else who'd been poorly seemed to manage to get there too. They were all talking and laughing about the performance. I noticed quite a few people glancing over at me and heard the words 'Jelly', 'sick', and 'ha, ha ha', quite audibly.

Out of the corner of my eye, I saw Cicily in a ridiculous Oscars-style evening dress clinging to Sandy and saying she felt weak.

I was lurking on the sidelines with Roobs. She was feeling responsible for the 'poisoning' incident and I was feeling responsible for the sick incident.

Myf and Sonja were both 'flirting' with Benji Butler – which involved having an arm wrestle while he cheered them on. Myf was managing to hold Sonja off for much longer this time as she had both arms down her way-too-big Nurse's outfit sleeve.

As all the members of **sO.M.G.!** were there for the party, Mrs Lilac suggested they do an impromptu concert for everyone. They set up on the stage and Cicily and Polly **leapt** up with them and started backing singing to their first number, 'Short Girl'. They sounded like a flock of seagulls having a row.

Short girl ooooooh . . .
sOMG!

Then a gaggle of **sO.M.G.!** groupies turned up and started screaming. When Sonja noticed that one of them was wearing a scarf with 'Benji' on it she tried to strangle her with it. But then she tuned in to the music that **sO.M.G.!** were playing. It wasn't *at all* to her taste.

Benji!!

She only liked rap.

She put her headphones on, turned up

Rubbish!

her rap so **LOUDLY** you could hear it above the din and left in disgust leaving Myf to take over the task of strangling the girl with the Benji scarf on.

The impromptu **sO.M.G.!** concert was getting a bit out of hand now and groupies were trying to climb up onstage, so Mrs Lilac suggested (very nicely) that they stop playing and maybe it would be better if **sO.M.G.!** left.

Oh for goodness sake! I'd been really looking forward to this party and now Sandy was leaving! Not that I cared as it was **Roger** I actually had a crush on and he was still there, surrounded by hysterical Year Eight kids demanding selfies with his tights.

I decided to approach him and see if he was feeling more forgiving towards my sick. Sandy and sO.M.G.! were leaving (with Cicily and Polly in tow) and I saw that Sandy was glancing over at me so I held his gaze (rather than show my ears in profile) and then did **LOUD** laughing with Roger.

HARH, HARH, HARH!
Don't be sick on me again, Jelly!!!!

'Course I won't,' I said, dragging Roobs with me to follow him along the corridor.

He said (from a safe distance), 'So how's it going with the bass? It's the Boxford's Got Talent competition next week, isn't it?'

'What?!' I shrieked.

'Oh my God!' cried Roobs.

'Next week!? We're not ready!'

'We'll have to cancel our entry,' Roobs said.

Then Myf came stomping along wearing the scarf with 'Benji' written on it and said:

'We're entering and that's that. Have you seen the competition?' she said, pointing along the corridor. 'We've got a really good chance!'

All along the corridor posters for the competition were lined up . . .

GRAROL SINGS THE BLUES
AND EVERYONE ELSE GETS THEM!
SPECIALLY THE FOX
Printed with gold leaf on velvet
THE NAUGHTY GIRLS*
*BUMP MY BUM!!
DANCE SPECTACULAR
BILLY RUMBLE
COMEDIAN
'I'm Funny.'
Sue, Julian, Cat 'n' Fats
FOLK COMBO
(Including animals and older people . . .)
BAND WITH NO
NAME
Bethany Iceland
HYPNOTIST
She'll hypnotise you with her BURNY eyes

And then at the very end . . .

I started laughing at the way Jay hadn't left enough room for the whole name . . . but then . . .

'Hold on! I don't believe it! You can't use that name, Roger – it's ours!!' I cried.

'You're called Jay and the Mould Breakers too, Jelly?' Roger said, nervously shielding himself again. 'That's a coincidence.'

'No it's not – Jay's stolen our name – he makes me sick!'

At the sound of the word 'sick', Roger made his excuses and hurried off.

'Right,' I said to the other two, 'I think we SHOULD enter! We're not going to be any worse than that lot.'

'Yeah! And we'll get all those boy groupies!'

'Yeah!' Roobs and I agreed.

-26-
Web Sight

We realised that if we really **WERE** going to enter Boxford's Got Talent in a week's time AND win then we'd better start rehearsing, so we went back to mine to have a meeting in the Faithful Club shed.

Sue, Julian, Cat 'n' Fats were rehearsing in the kitchen, Grarol was 'singing' in the living room and there was some kind of -noise- coming out of Jay's room too. The racket was pretty BAD.

'You're right, Jelly, we can't be worse than that!' Myf said.

We agreed we would stick with Myf's song 'Love Me Please' as we couldn't come up with anything better in the time. We just needed to get some instruments and learn them. We already had Roger's bass but it had a GIANT spider's web on it, which none of us was feeling brave enough to tackle . . .

'Oi! Girliewirlies!' Jay shouted through the window. 'Roger needs his guitar back!'

'Myf's using it!' I told him.

'Well, how come she's still playing a tennis racquet?' he sniggered. 'We need it! We're starting up our band again. We want some of what sO.M.G.! have got, some of those groupies!'

That's a pathetic reason to start a band. And, by the way, you're not allowed to call yourselves Jay and the Mould Breakers.

It doesn't make any sense – it's like
Myf and the Mould Breakers.

'Myf and Jay don't have anything to do with Mould. MOULD. Something you make a JELLY in?' I explained to them. 'Jelly and the Mould Breakers? Don't you get it?'

'Whatever,' Jay muttered. 'Anyway, Roger needs his bass back. **NOW!**'

'You're welcome to come and take it,' I said, pointing at the massive spider. Jay was even more frightened of spiders than me.

Pass it over.
No!
(trembling with fear)
(shaking with terror)

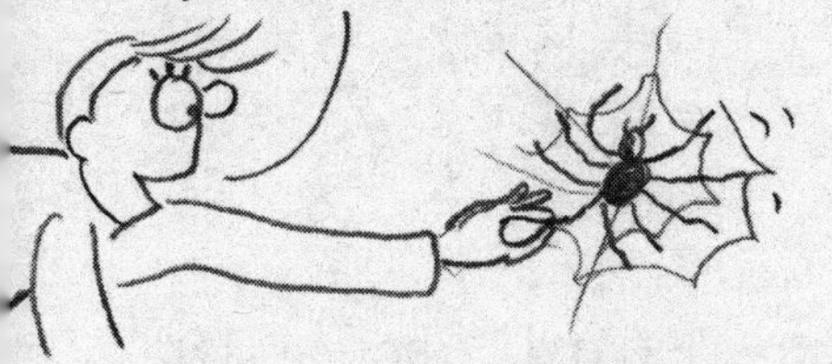

Oh, honestly, frightened of a little spider!

Don't kill it!

Roger scooped up the spider, stepped into the house into our downstairs loo and flushed the chain.

He'd flushed the spider down the loo!

I went completely off him. I thought he was supposed to be an animal lover!

But then I reasoned with myself – he was so nice in so many other ways – and I *had* got a crush on him – and, I mean, I ate sausages and stuff even though I really liked pigs (apart from Sandy). . .

Maybe the spider would swim through the pipes and cling on somewhere and then manage to climb back up through the plug hole or something? (As long as it wasn't when I was in the bath.)

Jay was saying, 'Heard about you vomiting on poor old Rog last night, Jelly!'

'Sorry, Roger,' I muttered.

'Oh, no worries, Jelly. You couldn't help it.'

His hair was all back in place again, which made me remember his wash bag with all the cosmetics in it.

'You're welcome to keep the bass for now, Jells,' he said. 'I can practise on my old one.'

He **winked** at me and did his handsome smile but it somehow didn't have the usual effect and I didn't go that **red**. I was still thinking about the poor spider.

–27–
Idiots

We spent the rest of the week rehearsing really **hard** every day after school for at least two minutes (exhausting!!) and Myf managed to learn one note on the bass guitar.

The rest of the time we worked on our image.

We had decided to go for an **80s** look and had all been raiding our mums' wardrobes for their teenage clobber.

Myf's mum had been a **huge** Madonna fan. Roobs's mum was a great admirer of Diana, Princess of Wales. And my mum used to be an electro-pop fan.

We also chose our **make-up** and decided to go for a **GLAM ROCK LOOK** in the facial department. We looked pretty **AMAZING**! Roobs said she knew someone in the band going on before us – 'Band With No Name' – and they had agreed to lend us their instruments. We were ready!!!

We planned one last rehearsal the night before the competition in the shed in FULL outfits and **make-up**.

'A one, a two, a one, two, three, four!' I shouted. Roobs did her drum intro on the biscuit tins and Myf started blasting out her one note.

Love, love me please,
Don't be a tease,
I'll always be true,
So plee-ee-ee-ease,
Love me please.
BISCUITS

Then Jay stuck his head through the window.

You can't do cover versions, idiots!

(Myfz.H and Roobz.M giggling hysterically even though Jay has called them idiots.)

'For goodness sake, you dorks!' Jay laughed. 'That's a <u>Bootles</u> song written by the greatest songwriters EVER – Lemon and McHearty!'

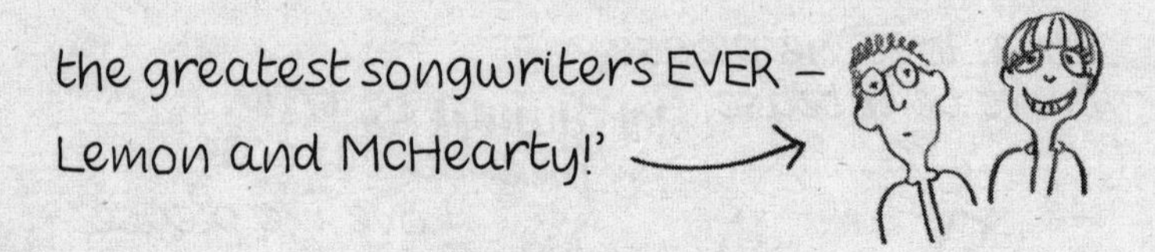

(Myf's third time ever going red.)

Myf explained that she thought it was a long-forgotten one-hit wonder from ancient times (1960s).

Then Jay took back Roger's guitar, checking it for spiders first.

-28-
Shut Up!

The next day we tried really hard to come up with an original song on the way to the town hall on the bus.

The wheels on the bus go round and round, round and round, round and ROUND!?

Whaat? What's wrong with it?

And we carried on trying to come up with songs backstage while the first few bands played. But it was no good! We kept just repeating whatever anyone onstage was saying or singing . . .

'Look,' I told Myf and Roobs, 'we can't go on – it's no good! We can't actually play and we haven't got a song! Don't bother changing into your outfits.'

Myf and Roobs started protesting but suddenly – they were announcing us –

'Thank you very much, Band with No Name! And now welcome to the stage Jelly and the Mould Breakers!'

Myf and Roobs dragged me on to the stage.

Come on, Jelly – they're clapping!

I stood quaking on the stage in front of the crowd of expectant faces and thought I should explain that we couldn't enter because we couldn't play and we hadn't got a song. **MEANWHILE** unbeknownst to me Myf had grabbed up Band With No Name's lead guitar and Roobs had **leapt** on to their drum stool.

I got as far as picking up the microphone and clearing my throat when there was this horrendous racket – Myf was strumming her one note and Roobs was bashing away on the drums behind me.

I couldn't look round because of my profile!

I yelled, 'I'm sorry, everyone, but we won't be able to play . . .'

(I noticed Sonja Perkins was sitting right at the front wearing her headphones.)

'We can't actually . . .' I continued, trying to be

heard above the racket, 'You see – SHUT UP!' I yelled to Myf and Roobs. *'SHUT UP! SHUT UP! SHUT UP!'*

Then Fatty ran onstage (Sue, Julian, Cat 'n' Fats were on next and were waiting in the wings).

SHUT UP, SHUT UP, SHUT UP!

Fatty echoed.

Only I knew he was also telling them to shut up – he hated heavy metal.

And on it went – the booming, *crashing* music, me shouting 'Shut up!' over and over again and Fatty echoing me each time . . . *Row-ru! Row-ru! Row-ru!*

Then Sonja stood up, took her headphones off and started dancing and joining in too . . .

SHUT UP, SHUT UP, SHUT UP!

Row-ru!
Row-ru!
Row-ru!
(Else I'll whack you-ou.)

And it went on like this . . .

SHUT UP,
SHUT UP,
SHUT UP!
Row-ru!
Row-ru!
Row-ru!
(Else I'll whack
you-ou.)

. . . until the audience, seeing Sonja as a very **COOL** person, all decided they liked it too and soon the whole hall was dancing.

I did notice that Myf seemed to have miraculously learnt another note and once she got it right it sounded OK, and Roobs's drumming, though a bit basic, wasn't sounding too bad either . . .

But then Mum came on and started to try to drag Fatty off.

Fattaaaay!! You traitor! You're in our folk combo, you idiot!! Come and put your Fair Isle tank top on NOW!

–29–

Feeling Ruff, Ruff, Ruff

I started edging off the stage, and was hurrying along the corridor when Sandy appeared out of the hall . . .

Jelly! That was amazing! It was so – original! I could never write a song like that – we just do cover versions. I mean, I don't like thrash rap usually but that was unbelievable!

You're joking? Oh look, I'm going home.

'No,' he said, grabbing my sleeve, 'you shouldn't.'

'But you don't understand – my family are all about to come on,' I explained.

'Jelleeeee! Jelleeee! Help!' It was Myf and Roobs running towards us.

'Anyway,' Sandy said, 'do you fancy going—'

But Sandy was drowned out by a marauding mob of screaming Year Eight girls coming after Myf and Roobs . . . and me!

Jellee!! . . .
I love Myf!!
Roobs is cool!!!
Jelleee and the Mould Breakers!!!

Just as they swamped us, Sonja appeared, shouting, 'Oi! Back off, you lot! Get in an orderly queue AFTER the show is finished else the girls won't pose for selfies with you.'

Sonja asked if she could manage us, and we said yes – else she might've whacked us, and anyway, she had perfect credentials for being a band manager.

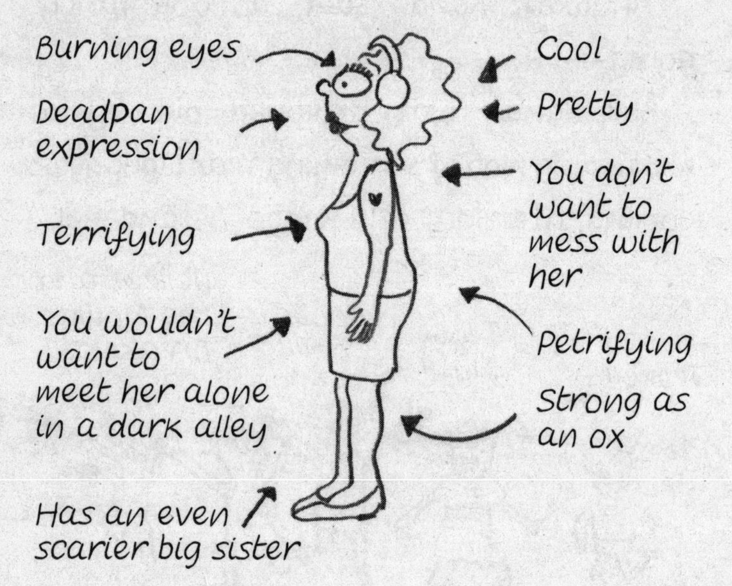

'C'mon,' Sonja said, 'let's go back in and watch the competition, not that we've got anything to be worried about.'

We all trooped back in and huddled at the back of the hall.

Sue, Julian, Cat 'n' Fats's Folk Combo weren't going down too well.

Then it was Grarol, who made a grand entrance.

Last, and also least, it was Jay and the Mold Breakers (the slight change in spelling did not appease me).

It was very, very, VERY **embarrassing** – but also very, very, VERY enjoyable. (And the fact that someone had changed 'Mold' to 'Wind' on their drum kit DID appease me!)

-30-
Jelly Legs

When the awards were presented we won 'BEST BAND' as well as 'MOST ORIGINAL SONG' for 'Shut Up (Else I'll Whack You)' by Jelly and the Mould Breakers Feat. Sonz P and FattsZFatzo, as well as being the overall winner of Boxford's Got Talent.

Despite the meanness of the audience towards my family, the judges awarded Grarol 'BEST ACT OVER FIFTY' (which meant she could tell everyone she was only fifty-one when she was actually seventy-five), Sue, Julian, Cat 'n' Fats's Folk Combo 'BEST ANIMAL ACT' (Mum felt she had achieved her dream and could happily go back to her ordinary life now) and Jay and the Mold Breakers the 'AUDIENCE PRIZE' due to Roger Lovely's ~~looks~~ talent.

So as overall winners we had to go on and sing again, and as is the tradition with Boxford's Got Talent, the other winners came on and sang with us.

So we were like a kind of FAMILY SUPERGROUP just for one night. We had to do two songs – the lyrics of 'Shut Up' were very easy to learn and I quickly made up another rap called 'Walk (Don't Talk)' Featz FattzZFatzo – knowing that Fatty would do EXCELLENT dancing and singing when anyone said the word 'walk' or anything that rhymed with 'walk'.

I improvised most of the rap (I really was *quite* good at it, though I say so myself) and the one note that Myf had learnt plus the other one she had chanced upon and Roobs's natural rhythm on the drums served us very well.

I'm talkin' with my friends,

And he's like, walk, don't talk,
Walk, don't talk.

Walk away, you dorks,
She's comin' wit' me.

He pops my cork,
He eats yogurt with a fork.

He's gonna walk wit' me,
Not talk at me.

(Rpt x 17)

And afterwards, as promised by our new manager, we posed for selfies for an hour.

(Sonja was excellent at making sure none of our new groupies took too long taking their snap.)

Sonja seemed to have lost all interest in Benji Butler now she was manager of J.M.B. (and had heard **sO.M.G.!**'s music) so Myf was happy.

Our dream of BILLIONS of boy groupies hadn't come true – they were *all* girls – but none of us cared.

However, right at the very back was one boy groupie – Sandy Blatch – and he asked me to pose for a selfie with him. Just me. He was just about to put his arm round me when Cicliy came beavering over.

Sandy! What are you doing?!
I'm taking a selfie with Jelly.
Can I be in it?
No, Cicily, you can't.
But . . . you're MY boyfriend!

'No, Cicily, I'm not,' Sandy said firmly. 'I let you boss me about because I was feeling confused and I thought Jelly didn't like me any more which made me a bit sad . . .

But then she stopped **looking** away when I looked at her and started staring at me and I knew she still liked me.'

'B-but . . .' Cicily stammered.

'Go away, Cicily . . .' he said firmly, and took his scarf from round her neck and put it back round my neck.

she pronounced threateningly, yanking her tartan scarf from Sandy's neck and almost strangling him. But there underneath her scarf was my scarf! Still firmly tied and still with egg on it. He hadn't taken it off even to wash it! Which was very unhygienic but quite romantic. ♡ ♡

Sandy held his phone aloft again and just before he took the photo, he said,

Jelly, look this way.

And I turned to him and he **kissed** me – right on the **lips**!!!!

Because he'd taken me by **surprise** I didn't have time to **WORRY** and I just **kissed** him back – just as the flash went off. It was very nice and my tummy did a little somersault, and my legs went . . . well – they went *jelly-ish*.

Then there was this huge *crash* behind us – Cicily had tried to photo bomb us but she'd fallen awkwardly and hurt her foot. She was making an **ENORMOUS** fuss and everyone was rallying round her and in all the confusion I lost Sandy.

-31-
Cute Again

Later that night my phone beeped. Sandy had sent me the selfie he'd taken with a little message

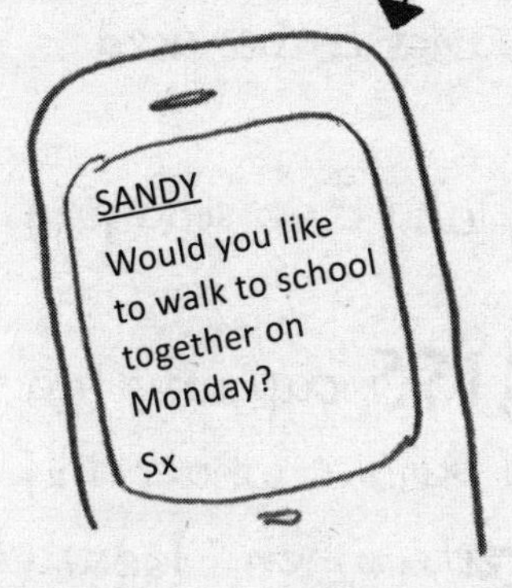

SANDY
Would you like to walk to school together on Monday?
Sx

Of course I went pink and my legs turned to jelly again, but I answered: 'Yes x'.

I'd learnt quite an interesting thing. Boys are sensitive too – and if you LOOK away when they look at you they think you don't like them but if you LOOK back at them for a bit longer than comes naturally (like I had to when I was trying not to display my ears in profile) . . .

. . . they think that you *might* possibly like them. And everyone wants to be liked – even boys.

I then spent quite a long time studying the photo.

My first proper **kiss** captured on camera – and d'you know what? My profile looked quite pretty when I looked happy. And my ears looked quite cute again.

My Early Years in Music

When I was fourteen, my friends and I started a punk band called The Sokitz (our 657th possible name). We made badges, posters, and screamed and yelled whilst banging biscuit tins with sticks for a few minutes.

It's really time for a reunion tour (we're all broke). But must just quickly learn some instruments first . . .